Leveling Up

Also by Jazzy Mitchell

Undertow

You Matter

Musings of a Madwoman

Lost Treasures

Leveling Up

Jazzy Mitchell

Leveling Up

By Jazzy Mitchell

ISBN (trade) 9781633040540
ISBN (ebook) 9781633040533

Launch Point Press
4804 NW Bethany Blvd, Suite I-2 #148
Portland, OR 97229

Editor: Toni Kelley
Cover Design: Michelle Brodeur

Blurb

Six years after completing her internship, Clarke Parson, a videogame graphic designer and animator, finds herself back in the orbit of Haboob Software's CEO, Fran Silvetti. Clarke contacts Fran to warn her that the game her company is developing was stolen from Clarke's computer by an ex-girlfriend after an acrimonious breakup. As Clarke is swept into a torrid affair with the fascinating CEO, she covets their time together, hoping Fran may someday return the love Clarke harbors for her.

Acknowledgments

Thanks to my family, friends, and colleagues—all helped me push through my blocks and listen to my characters' tales. Thanks to my wife, our three children, and my writing companion, Delilah. They've taught me how to be present in my life, so I don't miss the good stuff.

Thanks also goes to Desert Palm Press—Lee and Toni for their expertise with getting this book in publishable shape and Mich for the awesome cover art. I also want to thank those who read the rough versions, C.A. Farlow, Jane Alden, and Renee Young. Their feedback made a difference. Thanks also to the Minnesota Minions for their help with fleshing out some of the story's details—particularly Jessie Chandler, Judy Kerr, and MB Panichi. In addition, I am grateful for the support of a local writing group, the Portland Lesbian Writers Group (PoLeWG). Four of the polliwog writers, Patricia Hansen, Sandra de Helen, Kay Grey, and Jane Cuthbertson, were happy to discuss the book and help me with the plot points. And thanks must go to the leader of the polliwogs, Lori L. Lake. Her friendship and guidance have helped me in countless ways. She's a rockstar. My life is richer with her in it.

Dedication

Like many other writers, I found it hard to write during the COVID-19 pandemic. Thanks to the entry of Delilah into my life, I found my way back. Delilah is my one-year-old puppy—a five-pound Maltese/Shih Tzu mix. As soon as I held her one-and-a-half-pound body, she crawled into my heart space and made herself comfortable. She is my companion, my writing partner, and my mood-lifter. She makes me take breaks when I've stared at the computer screen for too long. She reminds me how to communicate through body language, and she rewards me with kisses for a good writing session. Her unconditional love reminds me that no matter what is happening outside my home, she will always remain my staunchest supporter.

Chapter One

THE BEGINNING OF THE REST OF HER LIFE

HURRYING DOWN THE STREET, Clarke Parson tries not to think about the fact that the wind chill is ten degrees below zero, or that her last meeting of the day isn't for two more hours, or that she is furtively looking around hoping to catch a glimpse of—no. She won't think of the name. She won't.

Clarke may not be able to control her dreams, but she can damn well control her wayward thoughts. It's been six fucking years, after all. When will these feelings fade? When will she be able to move on? When will she be able to walk down a street in Manhattan without hoping to somehow see—her?

No, she needs to keep her focus. This afternoon's meeting can set her up for the next few months, and knowing she'll have a steady paycheck will do wonders for controlling her stress levels. She loves what she does, loves working freelance, but it places the pressure of making money squarely on her shoulders. She knows she could secure a fulltime job with no problem at this point in her career, but she doesn't care to work for one company. She tries to beat back the thought that she doesn't want to eliminate any possibility of working on one of Haboob Software's projects. She frowns. It doesn't matter how good she is, or her meteoritic rise in the gaming industry, or the recognition she's received as a videogame graphic designer and animator, or the steady stream of projects she works on—none have created a bridge to cross the ravine created when she left Haboob.

So caught up in her thoughts, she nearly misses that she's striding past the Brightman-Cook building, Haboob Software's home base. Nearly. She can never pretend, even to herself, to be entirely oblivious to her surroundings, not whenever she is near here. Near her. Even as she navigates with head down and body huddled, Clarke finds herself searching with her peripheral vision for a known face. She finds one.

"Cap!" Harry exclaims as he grabs her arm.

Clarke's head shoots up in surprise. "Harry!" she responds as she's hauled close for a bear hug. She feels a wave of affection flow through her. Harry Toland is a lanky, dark-haired Irishman—with a hard-to-crack exterior and mushy interior. He's also the lead designer for Haboob Software. Once she passed all his tests, he became her closest friend while working as an intern at Haboob. God, to be as bright-eyed and bushy tailed as she was then. It feels like a lifetime ago.

They kept in touch after her internship with the company ended, at first, but as time passed and deadlines dogged their heels, they drifted away from one another. Nowadays, they exchange emails every so often. They haven't gotten together in about a year though, and Clarke feels guilt settle in her gut, knowing she could do more to keep their friendship alive. Wishing she had done more.

"We have to catch up. Dinner tonight? Say eight o'clock at that new Italian bistro on 47th and 7th?"

Clarke quickly agrees, silently vowing not to allow their relationship to wane again. As she walks away, Clarke swears someone is watching her. The prickling sensation up her spine tells her so. She does not look back.

***

After joining Harry at the restaurant, Clarke listens with a rabid hunger as Harry updates her without prompting on the happenings at Haboob Software. Clarke is grateful. She always wants to know how everyone is, even if she'd rather not ask directly. It's not as if she did anything wrong. In fact, she completed a successful internship, no small feat since Haboob Software is one of the largest and most distinguished videogame development companies in the world with a proven record of successful PC, console, and mobile videogames.

Once the server appears with their wine and takes their orders, Clarke orders herself to calm the fuck down and listen to what Harry's saying. Her heart is racing as she tries to focus on his words. She's distracted, as always happens when receiving information about the machinations around her former employment. Her thoughts always focus on one person, to the exclusion of all others. Harry waits until they're alone before picking up his narration.

"We've been working nonstop to develop *End of the World, the Greenhouse Effect* so we can release it for the Christmas season. That's the name of what's going to be the best game introduced this year. The designer's an up-and-comer. She came out of nowhere."

"What is that? Some kind of apocalyptic game? Shoot 'em up stuff? Or is it more speculative fiction and world-building?"

"More like science fiction, unfortunately. The central storyline is how humankind has affected the climate. The player has to make choices which may lead to an uninhabitable world or the healing of it. The graphics are sick. Reminds me of your style. Sig brought a good chunk of the graphics and animation to us, which is unusual. That's why we were able to fast-track it."

What Harry said rings in her ears, and she gasps. Her hands begin to tremble. "Who did you say?" she asks, her voice shaking.

"Sig Sassy. About nine months ago, she demanded an audience with La Silvetti. Luckily for her, the game was good enough to excuse her arrogance. She said she was working on it for years, and with the advanced stage it was in, we believed her. It's weird how we've never heard of her before. Said she was in Frankfurt for a few years, honing her skills." He cocks his head. "You look like you've seen a ghost. What's up?"

Clarke feels shockwaves rushing through her system. "Sig Sassy? Did you say Sig Sassy? Oh no." She leans forward, an urgent need to warn Harry washing through her. "Harry, you can't release that game. It will ruin the company—"

"Slow down, Clarke. What are you talking about?" Harry interjects, alarmed by Clarke's reaction.

Clarke feels alarmed, too. She knew Sig was jealous when she realized Clarke still harbored a raging crush on Fran Silvetti, the former creative director and present CEO of Haboob Software. What were the chances that her ex-girlfriend stole Clarke's videogame schematics and sold them to her former employer? Rather good, evidently.

Clarke takes a deep breath and exhales on a silent count of five to calm herself. "Harry, she's a crook. She stole that game from my laptop. I've spent the last eighteen months developing it for Runaway Games, and I was going to submit the rest of the animation next week." Clarke has freelanced as an animator for Runaway Games since she left Haboob Software. It allows her to work on a few projects at a time without being tied to a desk every day. "I can prove it. We had a huge blow out over a year ago, right before we broke up. I changed my passwords on everything, but she must have downloaded the story and game designs when I wasn't around."

"Jesus." Harry exhales. "If Sig doesn't own the rights..." He slouches in his seat, one hand rubbing the back of his neck. "Legal usually performs a background check when they draw up the agreements. Why didn't they catch it?"

"She knew all about the project. I'm sure she was able to cover her tracks. You have to stop the release." Clarke says again, intent on making him understand. "Tell me you haven't paid her anything."

"I wish I could. We paid an advance, not to mention the money that's gone into developing the game and advertising it. Everything's prepped." He gazes at Clarke. "Obviously, we'll have to change that so Sig doesn't get any more money or prestige. When Fran gets through with her, she'll never be able to sell another game, or even produce one on her own. She'll be pushed out of the industry."

"I'll send you the proof. Timestamps and schematics. Email exchanges with the design team. Even my early storyboards and artwork." Clarke can't help cringing. Some of it is amateurish.

Harry takes an inelegant gulp of his red wine and leans back against his chair. "You have to send the work product directly to Fran. Today."

Clarke feels lightheaded at the thought and begins to shake her head emphatically. "No way. No way. I won't do it. It has to come from you, Harry."

"Clarke. Come on. You're overreacting here. You need to send it to her. We don't have time to send it up the chain." Clarke ignores Harry's reasonable request. She doesn't want to hear it.

"Nope. No can do. Not gonna happen. I haven't spoken to that woman in six years. What do you suppose she's going to think if she gets an email from me unexpectedly like this?" Clarke asks before finishing off her drink. "I'll tell you. She'll wonder just what the hell I'm up to. She'll immediately believe I'm trying to sabotage her in some way." Clarke waves her hands around as agitation gets the better of her. "And let's not even get into how many ways I can be fired for sharing that stuff. You know the deal."

"So tell Dirk the Jerk what happened. He'll be thrilled to partner with us. We have the workforce, and we'll incorporate the work you've done on it. Call him now."

With a sigh, Clarke hits Dirk Waters' number. He's the creative director for Runaway Games. As soon as she hears Dirk's voice, her heart speeds up. "Dirk, it's Clarke. I just found out that *Gassed Out* was sold out from under us to Haboob Software nine months ago." She holds the cell phone away from her ear, grimacing at the loud curses. She can see from Harry's expression that he can hear each word.

"Dirk. Dirk. Hey. Wait. Calm down. Listen." Clarke looks up at the ceiling, pressing her lips together as she waits for Dirk to run out of steam. "Okay. I know it seems bad, but we can come back from this."

As a new flood of loud curses causes Clarke to hold the phone away from her ear again, Harry snaps his fingers and moves his hand in a gimme motion. She hands the cell phone to him.

"Hello, Dirk. It's Harry from Haboob Software. I know you're upset. You have every reason to be. I know your company has been developing the game for a lot longer than we have. It seems we were both duped, but we're going to sort this out. Come meet me tomorrow at nine. Yes, at the Brightman-Cook building. We'll get everything settled and on track. Don't worry. If it weren't for Clarke, we'd both be in a heap of trouble. Yes, she's a keeper. Bye-bye."

Tucked in the corner of the booth chair, Clarke watches Harry as he places her phone on the table, a serious look on his face. "Back to the other matter. Send the information to Fran tonight. She doesn't hate you. In fact, she knows you're a respected animator. You've made quite a name for yourself in a relatively brief period of time, and she's kept track. She'll know the information is legitimate, and I'll have her be part of the meeting tomorrow morning."

Clarke places her head in her hands, not sure what to do. It overwhelms her to think Fran has kept track of her career. *Why would she after practically shooing me out the door after my internship ended? Why didn't she offer me a job?* Clarke keeps silent, her jumbled thoughts creating enough noise to make up for it.

"All right, how about this?" Harry cajoles. "Send it to Fran and to me. I'll mention that we had dinner, and this came out. She'd believe you anyway, but I'll emphasize how you've been developing the game for over a year and tell her about the meeting."

"But then she'll know my email address." Clarke can't help the whining tone of her voice.

Harry smirks. "So? I've told you before that she believes you're the one who got away. All that talent, and she didn't realize it until you were gone." Clarke watches the smile fade on Harry's face as he becomes serious. "Come on, Cap. Just do it. It's the only way we can keep on schedule while taking care of Sig." A twinkle in Harry's eyes warns Clarke that he's about to tease her. "Besides, what do you think is going to happen? She'll start spamming you?"

They stare at each other. Clarke throws a wadded napkin at him. "Fine, you bastard. I'm so glad we bumped into each other." She mentally stomps her foot even as she capitulates.

"Me, too," Harry singsongs as he waves the server over to order another round of drinks.

Recognizing she needs to do this does not calm her. The thought of contacting Fran for any reason whatsoever scares the shit out of her. It doesn't matter that it's really her fault Sig was able to steal the designs from her laptop after watching Clarke type in her laptop password one too many times. It doesn't matter that Clarke's desire to help Fran outweighs her fears. No amount of calm, rational thinking can wipe away her growing apprehension. Nevertheless, she has agreed to tell Fran, and Clarke intends to follow through.

Deciding to walk home after she leaves Harry, Clarke thinks about the ramifications of contacting Fran. Over the past six years, she's avoided Haboob Software and Fran Silvetti, to the detriment of her career. She knows she's talented enough to work on their video games, but she's remained afraid to be within Fran's vicinity. Afraid Fran will notice her. Afraid she won't. It was one thing to be a silly intern, undeserving of Fran's time for even a single moment. It's quite another for Clarke to be successful and yet remain disregarded by Fran. It would be quite humiliating, not to mention soul-destroying.

On the night Sig ended their relationship, she'd mocked Clarke's unrequited feelings for Fran. Sig wasn't supposed to ever find out about them, but she'd pieced the clues together. The journal filled with poems Clarke had written, detailed enough for Sig to guess they were about Fran. The laptop file filled with handwritten notes she'd scanned—most were scribblings Fran left for Clarke during her internship, providing feedback or directives for different projects. The final nail in the coffin was her laptop password: blue-eyed Devil. The blowback was horrific.

"So, this is why you don't want to move in with me? You're still lusting after that frigid bitch? You realize she'll never give you the time of day. You were nothing to her when you were her intern, and by now I'm sure she doesn't even remember your name. You're nothing to her. It's pathetic that after all these years, you're still carrying a torch for her." A mean smile crossed Sig's Nordic features, shadows from the lamp obscuring her eyes. She stood in the middle of the room, hands on her hips.

"What? I don't know what you're talking about." Clarke closed the apartment door, grasping the bag full of food from a nearby Mexican restaurant. Glancing at her laptop, she saw it was open, Gassed Out schematics on the screen. She could have sworn she'd locked the computer before she left to pick up their food.

"Don't act like you don't know what I'm talking about." Sig strode toward Clarke, who took a step back. She stopped in front of Clarke, towering over her. "You're in love with Fran Silvetti, and don't even try to deny it. It was cute for a while, the way you'd rhapsodize over her talent when talking about her. I figured it was hero worship, a good old power crush, but it's more than that. You've fed it for years, and I'm not gonna stick around in a dead-end relationship while you live in fantasyland. I'm outta here." She picked up a bag Clarke hadn't noticed near the door. "I'd give you your key back, but you never gave me one. Guess I should have figured it out then." With a last sneer, Sig left with an emphatic slamming of the door.

It took Clarke a bit of time to catch up to what happened. She sank into the couch, blinking back tears. Her instinct to run after Sig, to call Sig, to somehow get her back—all faded when she noticed the documents pulled up on the screen. They were of internal memos and scanned messages from her time at Haboob. Closing them out, she stayed her hand while gazing at a photo of Fran from a few months ago. She was looking at the camera, a slight smile gracing her pink-stained lips. The royal blue sweater she wore emphasized her light-blue eyes. Her face seemed so animated, as if she were about to reveal a valuable secret. Clarke stared at the photo for a long time before shutting down her computer and spending the rest of the night avoiding any thoughts of Fran or Sig. She didn't think about the accusations. She didn't think about how odd it was that her laptop was open and in use. She didn't think about the mystery of why the Gassed Out *program was running. If she had taken the time, perhaps she could have guessed what Sig was planning.*

Beyond the personal implications of Fran dismissing her as an insignificant former intern, Clarke can think of several ways Sig's betrayal can sink her career. After all, she's supposed to safeguard any work product she has on her computer, not allow a jealous ex-lover to steal it. Sig's treachery was designed to embarrass her on multiple levels. If other companies find out, they may not believe she'll safeguard their projects. They may not want to hire her. They may believe she's negligent, untrustworthy, and amateurish. Clarke has no way to refute such beliefs.

Against all the fears she holds for the impending fallout, Clarke feels a duty to warn Fran. Although Fran is the CEO of a large development company, Haboob remains susceptible to lawsuits for releasing a video game when they've failed to secure the story's intellectual rights. Runaway Games owns the rights, and Haboob will have to come to some type of accord with them. Clarke shakes her head, a sick feeling setting up camp in her stomach. Runaway Games is a small development company with no hope of remaining in business if Haboob fights them for the rights to release the game. Even though Runaway Games is the proper owner, they have limited funds. A legal battle will push them into bankruptcy. It can't happen. So, Clarke has no choice but to contact Fran. She won't give Sig the satisfaction of damaging Fran's career.

Two hours later Clarke sits in her apartment staring at the computer screen. She has authored a simple email and attached her work product.

Hi.

It came to my attention today that a former acquaintance, Sig Sassy, stole work product off my laptop and sold it to your company for development. I have worked with Runaway Games for the past eighteen months to develop Gassed Out, *or as your company calls it,* End of the World, the Greenhouse Effect. *Attached are my drawings, storyboards, graphics, and schematics for the game. Harry will be meeting with Dirk tomorrow morning to figure out how to salvage this situation and combine the work done by both companies. I'm sure he'll be able to provide you with more details.*

I suspect you will find the perfect way to reward Sig for her duplicitous actions.

Clarke Parson

She doesn't use Fran's name since she doesn't have permission to be so familiar. She wouldn't dream of taking such a liberty without permission. Hitting the "send now" button, Clarke closes her eyes as relief washes through her. Who knew sending Fran an email would be more labor-intensive than the designs she's completed during countless hours to animate the game?

It's done now. Fran may be reading the email and looking at all the attachments at this moment. She may be contacting Harry to find out what he knows. He may be relating their dinner and Clarke's realization of the theft from her computer. She has no problem imagining various scenarios unfolding. She has no problem visualizing Fran's outrage and condemnation for Sig's actions and Clarke's stupidity.

For several months, after she had walked away from Haboob Software and from Fran, Clarke took pains to watch her walking in or out of the Brightman-Cook building. She also perused the newspapers, magazines, websites, and television for the chance to see her. Yet seeing Fran made Clarke feel worse. The reality of no longer having the right to interact with her ripped Clarke's heart to shreds.

Clarke had reacted in an extreme fashion. She began to turn to the next page, click to another website, and change the channel whenever she saw Fran. Clarke realized she was overreacting. However, she no longer allowed herself the privilege of staring at Fran. It was too painful. Over the years, Clarke become quite good at denying herself the pleasure of even thinking about Fran for longer than a conversation. In her weaker moments, she scoured the Web to find photos of Fran, downloading them into a file. Nausea rolls over her as she realizes Sig must have seen all of them in the computer folder, organized by date and labeled with the locations.

If she's honest, Clarke must admit that a large reason why she has allowed her relationship with Harry to fade is due to her inability to control the hunger she feels when news about Fran enters their conversations. After all these years, Clarke must admit defeat against her heart's campaign to be heard. Banning Fran from her thoughts, from her sight, has not helped Clarke to move on. It has only made her ache for Fran's presence even more. The truth is that forbidding herself permission to think of Fran is akin to telling herself to stop eating. She just becomes weaker and weaker the longer she denies herself.

Of course, giving herself permission to think of Fran doesn't mean she'll run into her office to stare at the woman. However, Clarke doesn't need to take such pains to avoid her, either. This sequence of events can act as a catalyst for her to process her feelings and move on.

A few days after sending Fran the game information, Harry calls Clarke to update her. As anticipated, all hell has broken loose. Fran has been on a rampage. They were able to form a partnership with Runaway Games, and everyone is clocking extra hours to incorporate the work completed by both companies. Clarke knows about the collaboration since Dirk told her about the meeting as soon as he returned from it. He was ecstatic.

"We're going to be rich, Clarke. Rich. Not to mention what a boost we'll get by having our name associated with Haboob. I'm so happy that I'm not even going to fire you for allowing someone to steal all that information from your computer. Good thing you found out before it was too late to do anything about it."

Serendipity has saved Clarke's job and dignity. It's also allowed her to reenter Fran's world, if only in this small way. Dirk has indicated that she's to finish the work she was doing and submit it to both him and Harry. She'll finish her part in a matter of days.

After she finishes the project, Clarke will contact Harry to schedule another dinner or at least drinks. No longer will she shy away from everyone and everything associated with Fran. She hasn't moved on because she hasn't allowed herself to deal with these feelings. It's time for Clarke to grow up. Perhaps if she examines her feelings, if she stares down her heart directly and sternly admonishes it for its unrealistic dreams, she'll be able to deal with the fact that she may not ever become a true part of Fran's life. This entire mishap has opened the door to a collaboration with Haboob, but that doesn't guarantee any future projects with them. Best to be thankful for the outcome and not expect anything else to develop. That way she won't have her hopes dashed and her heart broken again once she completes the project.

It's worth a try.

Chapter Two

THE ONE WHO WALKED AWAY

EVERY DAY, FRAN WAKES before the sun rises. It's as if her internal clock is perpetually set for five a.m. Sometimes she lies under the warm blankets before rising, allowing her mind to wander. Her best ideas have revealed themselves to her drowsy mind during these early hours, before the day rushes in, and it is during these hazy times that she allows her mind to dwell on the one who walked away.

How many times has she indulged in ridiculous, impossible, forbidden thoughts? Yet she cannot find it within herself to stop them. It is her only indulgence these days. In her mind, she imagines seeing her former intern again, of feeling that skin under her lips or gazing into revealing eyes. Oh yes, she has warmed many a chilly morning with thoughts of the one person who walked away without a backward glance. The heat in those chocolate eyes hinted at depths banked by propriety, professionalism, and fear. It is a cruel cliché. She fell for the young, heterosexual, brilliant intern with a promising future, emphasis on young. Underlined by heterosexual. Fran knew she was playing with fire, so she doused it with a bucket of reality. Taking her to her bed would ruin Clarke in too many ways to count. It was unfortunate to find she had feelings—passionate, amorous feelings—for Clarke. She refused to acknowledge them to herself, to Clarke. No, she had to send her away.

Fran tried not to dwell on how easy it was for Clarke to leave with a personal recommendation and a gentle shove out the door. She didn't ask for a job, and Fran didn't offer one. Fran didn't offer good wishes or sad smiles or any type of see-you-later. She treated it like a non-event, as she did with any other intern leaving the company after finishing their term, but no matter how many times she told herself that Clarke was not special, her heart didn't believe it.

Nevertheless, she did her best not to look back or feel regret or miss her. She knew she had to move on. Most people forgot all about Clarke. She was another intern who left the company to forge a career. No one uttered her name, and life went on. New projects filled her mind, and Fran focused on maintaining her reputation of running one of the best video development companies in the industry. Few people know that she's kept track, proud and bereft, of Clarke's meteoritic rise within the business.

Harry knows. He is one of those few people she trusts, and he has taken special pains to inform her how Clarke always perks up when he mentions her name. It was during one of these conversations that he accidently-on-purpose let slip how Sig Sassy had the opportunity to steal the schematics of what Runaway Games calls *Gassed Out*. It turns out the young, heterosexual, brilliant intern is not so hetero after all. Fran nearly fell out of her chair when the importance of that little nugget settled over her.

When Clarke reentered her life in this startling way, Fran wasn't sure how to feel. It is hard to believe—Clarke looking out for her, taking care of her without expecting anything in return except blame after someone she trusted hacked into her computer. Oh, she can claim to have given her the head's up because it was the right thing to do, but Fran knows the fault must land squarely on her lap for not completing her due diligence for the intellectual rights before applying for the development and console licenses. She knew the idea came from a fanfiction story which had gone viral, and she believed Sig Sassy when she claimed to be the author. She was careless, and it nearly cost her career and the livelihood of her employees—hundreds of people who relied on her. No, regardless of Clarke's claims, Fran now understands she's not the only one harboring feelings. The possible fallout for Clarke's unwitting role in this is too great for her to take the chance of revealing the truth about Sig Sassy unless she cares for Fran.

Clarke's decision to protect her when normally no one dares gives her hope. Everyone assumes Fran can fend for herself, that any attempt to fight her battles is a gross insult. It's not true, though. Everyone needs help at times, and in Fran's position, she wears a large bull's eye every day. She usually must fend for herself, but Clarke has proven an unflagging and unending loyalty to her that she never expected.

That loyalty would have continued unnoticed yet potent, if the timing were different, if Haboob weren't so close to its release deadline. Luckily, Harry bumped into Clarke, which led to dinner, which led to the revelation that one Sig Sassy, their supposed cash cow and originator of this year's best video game, is a fraud. Fran will forever be grateful. Grateful to Harry for persuading her, grateful to Clarke for sending the information, even grateful to that duplicitous Sig Sassy, since it was her illegal actions which provided Fran with an opportunity, one she will optimize.

Remembering the past week, Fran smiles, a tenderness she's not used to feeling sweeping through her. She saw her. Clarke. What a welcome sight. Always so animated. So vivacious and filled with energy. She wears her emotions on her face. In her eyes. Those eyes that used to tell her so much. Fran's hands fist the sheets as her eyes flutter closed. Even now, she remembers those chocolate eyes, how she could find a wealth of emotion directed at her. She wants to see those eyes again, and not from a distance, not directed at Harry or at New York traffic or at her office window. If she is ever going to get Clarke back in her life, now is the time for grand gestures.

Does she want to take the risk? Does she want Clarke back in her life? Does she want to acknowledge how much she has missed her former intern? Yes to all. She might not admit it to anyone else, but she is disappointed in herself for her cowardly inaction. She is aware that she might never have reached out to Clarke, not knowing how and not believing it would be well-received. Now she knows better.

Dull light sifts through the drawn curtains. It is time to face the day. Fran shivers in the cool air as she rises and wraps her robe around her body with sure hands, an idea forming in her mind. Now that they have met with Runaway Games and ironed out an agreement, she will have more time to devote toward finding the perfect way to reach out to Clarke.

What can she do to impress Clarke? Obviously glamour, money, fame—none of those impress her. Yet something must have affected Clarke enough to want to protect her, some sort of tenuous connection. None of the artificial, transient riches one may find at the top of the gaming world, though. No, Clarke never succumbed to the allure of success other than a rich feeling of accomplishment, of seeing her work integrated into the game. It's possible that Fran's achievements attracted Clarke, that their similar work ethic and ability to implement observations of human behavior created a bond between them all those years ago. Dare she hope that bond remains? Material things might not capture

Clarke, but actions do. Clarke has always noticed even the smallest ones and interpreted them with an eerie accuracy.

Pausing by the window, Fran looks out at the dull morning, weak rays reflecting off the pavement. Fran has gone down this path many times before. She's played the game of what ifs and should haves. It would not have taken much to contact Clarke after she left, but she never did, and over time the possibility became a comforting, often revisited fantasy. That was all. It is ironic, really. Fran is a woman of action, yet it is Clarke who took action to protect Fran. *Actions do speak so much louder than words*, Fran muses. It is time for Fran to take definitive action.

Decision made, Fran studies her reflection in the window critically. If she decides to do this, she must reach out in a way that will invite the opportunity for interaction so that she can determine whether Clarke might be willing to return to the fold. Oh, not as an employee. Certainly, she has grown into her own over the years since she left Haboob Software. Nor does Fran wish for Clarke to feel diminished in any way. Fran wants to create a new dichotomy, a new type of interaction. She must show Clarke that she admires how far she's advanced in her career. What's more important is her respect for Clarke's personal choices—choosing to leave, choosing to freelance, and choosing to extend herself when she felt it was the correct course of action.

I need to show her that I care about her. That I want to know who she is. That I see her. What will reach her? Impress her? Invite her to respond? She is a hard-working graphic designer and animator. Her tools are decisive action coupled with expressive graphics and strong storylines. She notices the smallest detail and can recreate it through her characters. I will mirror her and hope she understands.

Tapping her lower lip with a finger, Fran decides she must do more than publish a public thank you. Fran's favor is weighty enough to cause others to trust whomever she favors. Others will seek Clarke out once Fran indicates her approval.

She needs to do more than that. It needs to be something more personal. She imagines Clarke's visage gazing back at her through the window, and wonders what will reach her. If she can show Clarke that she has taken an interest in her, it may be enough to bridge their time apart. The years of loneliness and loss. Although she may not know anything about Clarke's personal life, she well remembers the first day they met. Clarke had handed her examples of her collegiate projects from when she attended the New York Film Academy. Fran still has them. She's tracked Clarke since she walked away six years ago. Certainly, she can track down the rest of her projects from her graduate work. Maybe even her undergraduate assignments.

Fran thinks haughtily, *I know everyone in the industry. I can do anything.* It will not take much to use her contacts to gather information. Smiling to herself, Fran nods before turning away. She is going to seduce Clarke Parson using knowledge, and hopefully action. Lots of action. Fran shivers at the thought.

Turning away from the window, she listens to the silent apartment. So empty without her daughter. Elaine's decision to live on campus is understandable, even if Fran tried hard to persuade her daughter to remain at home. She knew it was a losing proposition. This is Elaine's time to explore and experiment and expand. During her college years in the city, Fran has no doubt that Elaine will make lifelong friendships, figure out what career she wishes to pursue, and discover which road she wants to walk. Of course, all of that may change later, but what excites Fran is that Elaine has begun her journey into adulthood.

Leaving her room, Fran descends the stairs and makes her way into the kitchen to make coffee and toast. She wonders whether Clarke would like her home. It's a co-op on the Upper West Side she's owned for about twelve years. It's a three-bedroom, two-and-a-half bath corner space with a terrace and magnificent views of the Hudson River. She was lucky to snag it at the end of the Great Recession. Although the economy's downturn negatively affected her industry, like so many others, she'd saved enough money to purchase the apartment through a short sale. Now her home is worth millions, and the board is picky about who it approves to purchase any of the units. With Elaine at school, her home feels big and cold. She doesn't like it. She can only hope that soon Clarke will breathe new life into this empty space.

***

It takes some time to get the gift ready. It is not a task she would hand off to an assistant. No, this requires her individualized touch. The stakes are too high to delegate any aspect of it to someone else. She knows, deep in her bones, that this is her last chance at finding happiness. The years apart have taught Fran much about herself. Others may believe her heartless, to be a ruthless businesswoman, one honed by the challenges a woman faces in a predominantly male industry, but it was a carefully crafted ruse which kept most from getting too close to her. She can count on her fingers the people she trusts, those she socializes with outside of work, those she can relax with after a long day. Once upon a time she'd wished for Clarke to become another trusted person, but the circumstances made that impossible. Those circumstances have changed.

Leaning her head back against the office chair, Fran allows her eyes to close for a moment. It's late. The launch for *End of the World, the Greenhouse Effect* is in two weeks, and she is determined to live up to her reputation of having it be a splashy, memorable affair. Brainstorming gave way to implementation of several interesting ways to impress the overall theme of the game—appreciating nature and making choices which will protect the planet instead of continuing to ravage it for resources and riches. Although Haboob Software develops games, the money comes from Brightman-Cook. It's fortunate she's on good terms with the game publishing company.

She wants to finish this grand gesture, this special project for Clarke, and get it to her before the video game's release. Fran knows Clarke will be at the launch since she developed much of the storyline and graphics. What Clarke doesn't realize is how prominently her name will be splashed across the board. It is unusual for a contract worker to receive credit for any of the work completed. Fran decided to ignore that industry standard once she saw proof that the game design was entirely Clarke's idea. When she compared her company's documents to what Clarke provided them, it was clear how much work Clarke completed—the game design, the narrative, and many of the character graphics remained the same, if not quite as polished. Giving Clarke the credit she deserves ought to help her secure enough projects to push her to the next level, similar to if not more than the amount of exposure she received when Fran's interviews leading to the ramp up of the release were published. If Clarke desires, she can attach herself to any of the large development companies as part of an in-house development team. In fact, if she so chooses, she can become a creative director or lead designer instead of continuing with freelance work.

Reviewing her work, a slow smile spreads across her face. She's done. It's ready. Smoothing her hands over the gift, she infuses it with her hopes and dreams, her forbidden fantasies. This is an offer for a new beginning. Although she doesn't know how Clarke will react, she knows Clarke will understand how much time and effort went in to creating this offering. She'll at least contact Fran to acknowledge she received it. Oh, but Fran will be ready, and she'll get to see Clarke again at the launch. Perhaps before then. Either way, Fran will make the most of this opportunity to reconnect with her. She is going to get the girl. And this time she will not watch her walk away.

Calling for her assistant, she arranges to have the gift delivered to Runaway Games. She knows Clarke is working out of their company building during the lead up to the launch. Since it's a smaller development company, they oversee more of their advertising and marketing duties themselves instead of outsourcing like Haboob does. Clarke is no doubt helping with the emails and web design, even though those aren't really her job. She's the first to roll up her flannel sleeves and jump into the thick of whatever task needs to be completed.

She'll never forget the first time she witnessed Clarke offering help outside her assigned job. They were working on a tennis video game, and the actor scheduled for motion-capture had to cancel. Clarke jumped in, offering to act out the scenes. Turns out she played competitive tennis in college. Knowing what a hassle it would be to reschedule the studio time, Fran allowed for the substitution. It was the best decision she'd made for that game.

When Clarke appeared in the mo-cap suit, Fran lost her breath. She could see every inch of Clarke in incredible definition. The girl was toned. Somehow, she kept in shape, and Fran had a challenging time keeping her prurient thoughts in check. They decided to add facial and finger markers before having Clarke act out several scenes for them. For the entire day, she got to watch Clarke move, all under the guise of professionalism. Her blossoming lust was anything but. The fluidity of her movements displayed her athleticism, her knowledge of the game, and her physical endurance. Fran had to censor her randy thoughts several times throughout the session, often chastising herself for allowing her gaze to wander. If she caught an employee ogling someone that way, she would fire that person after a thorough dressing down. She was ashamed of herself. The most important lesson of the day was recognizing the scheduled actor could not have pulled off the needed movements with the assurance of a true athlete. They would have lost time and money. Clarke was a godsend, and Fran made sure her company paid Clarke for her double duty.

With a loud exhalation, Fran blinked away the recollection, one of many she treasures. She'll have time for such memories later, when she first awakens and can fantasize that the unforgettable woman is lying next to her. She didn't get to the top of her industry by woolgathering, and she refuses to have others discover her sitting idly in her office. She pulls up the action list on her screen, straightening her shoulders as she dons her glasses. It's time to get back to work.

Chapter Three

SPECIAL DELIVERY

HEARING HER DESK TELEPHONE ring, Clarke eyes it curiously. "This is Clarke," she says. She doesn't usually work in the Runaway Games offices, but with two weeks to go until launch, it's easier to coordinate with the team when she's in person. She also isn't as likely to become distracted by the various daydreams she can't seem to stop when she's alone. Her mind loves to run possible scenarios of what will happen when she sees Fran again. She knows it will happen at the launch party for *Gassed Out*. She shakes her head. *No, no. It's* End of the World, the Greenhouse Effect *now.*

"You have a package up front."

Saving her work, she locks her computer before hopping up from her seat and strolling from the bullpen to the front of the building. She can use the excuse to stretch her legs. Since Sig Sassy was exposed and Fran publicly thanked Clarke for her role in uncovering Sig's duplicity, she has received several invitations to work on lucrative projects. Video games. Movies. Even a sci-fi television series. As if by saving Haboob Software from an embarrassing argument of "who owns the story rights" and Runaway Games from certain bankruptcy, she has earned the trust of those in the know. She'd feared they would blame her since Sig stole the information from her laptop, but everyone's treating it as if she were the victim in the data hacking. Consequently, Clarke has been working hard to take advantage of the unexpected abundance of new projects and a few follow up projects for *End of the World, the Greenhouse Effect* she received after the two companies joined efforts not only to get the game out to the masses but also to ban Sig from the industry. The irony does not escape her. Her career has completed a cycle, beginning and ending at the feet of Fran Silvetti.

Of course, she has changed. She's different than the idealistic, naïve intern of six years ago. Still, Clarke feels as if she owes her career to Fran with her baptism through fire, that indoctrination to the gaming world while Fran was her taskmaster, and then her subsequent and surprisingly lucrative freelancing career as first a graphic designer and later as an animator.

Fast-forward six years later, and it seems she still owes her career to Fran. In a startling departure from her normal behavior, Fran wrote a letter to the editor for *Time Magazine*, published in conjunction with an interview, regarding the new video game. She condemned Sig Sassy and lauded Clarke's willingness to come forward once she discovered the deception, saving Runaway Games and Haboob Software. That endorsement has served as a green light for everyone else within the industry to trust Clarke. She understands this is Fran's way of thanking her for the warning. She has no doubt that Fran knew exactly what she was doing, knew that her praise would help Clarke professionally. And it has.

Not that she hasn't been successful. Clarke has worked her way up over the years, getting larger projects and winning more prestigious positions at more reputable companies. However, Sig's betrayal has catapulted her forward. People are accessing her website and requesting meetings to collaborate on projects. It feels good. More than good.

This week she's dug deep into the writing skills she honed while in college to create some advertisements for the upcoming launch. She's already updated the Runaway Games website, adding a countdown, various photos of behind-the-scenes, animation of each major character, and now the write-ups for each character, the overall story arc, and the fun activities which will occur at the launch. She has coordinated with Haboob to make sure they don't post conflicting information, and they've agreed on what to post. Clarke's volunteered to keep track of social media and update the various platforms up to the day of launch. As usual, she's taking on too much, but who needs sleep, anyway? This game has changed her life. She's opened the door to being in the same room as Fran and maybe even collaborating with her again. She's attracting some huge, lucrative projects. Even this project has become much more profitable with the new partnership. Besides the uptick in cool swag, she always brokers a royalty residual in her contracts, which acts as her coffee fund. With Haboob's reach and status, she'll be earning a hell of a lot more than coffee money. In fact, she'll have to figure out how best to invest it. *Maybe this will be a good excuse to call Dad, start rebuilding the bridge I burned when I refused to move home.*

Rolling her shoulders as she rounds the corner, Clarke stops in front of a large box with her name on it. At her questioning look, the receptionist tells Clarke that a messenger delivered it. Shrugging, Clarke hefts the box back to her desk while trying to guess what it is.

Taking a pair of scissors, Clarke uses one of the blades to slide over the packing tape covering the seam of the box. Pulling the tape off, Clarke opens the box to find a wrapped package inside. Carefully removing the gold cloth paper, Clarke gasps at what she sees: a dark, blood-colored, leather computer case with her initials embossed in gold on the front. She runs shaking fingers over the golden letters CAP before lifting the gift from the box and unzipping it. Inside sits a top-of-the-line laptop.

Sinking into her chair, Clarke reverently removes the computer and plugs it in. Booting up the system, she immediately realizes the gift-sender loaded it with helpful computer software. She lets out a low whistle. Icons for Unity, Unreal Engine, Maya, MotionBuilder, Faceware, Blender and several other graphic, animation, and audio programs litter the screen, along with the more ordinary programs which people use, such as Microsoft Office, virus and spyware protection, the full adobe creative suite, and Canva. Clarke laughs, overjoyed by this unexpected boon. Leaning back in her chair, she sits stunned, staring at the computer.

Realizing she has been mooning over this gift in a relatively public area for much too long, Clarke looks around furtively. Clarke is sitting at a computer set up in a large, open room. Most people have headphones on as they clack away on their laptops or keyboards, eyes flittering over multiple screens. Nevertheless, privacy is at a premium. Normally, Clarke's able to tune out her surroundings and focus on her screens, relegating the rest of the world to a background blur while she works. That doesn't mean someone won't notice her staring at her new laptop like a moony-eyed, lovesick techie. Which she absolutely is. This gift is sick in the best way. She can't think of anyone who would have sent her this treasure chest chock-full of expensive tech. Certainly no one from Runaway Games. Maybe from Haboob, which leaves two possibilities—Fran and Harry.

"You buy a new laptop?" The voice jogs Clarke out of her thoughts, nearly giving her a heart attack. She was so absorbed in her thoughts that she didn't hear anyone approach her desk. Turning her head, she sees Terry Strand looking with interest at the computer. Terry whistles in appreciation, eyes shining with envy while studying the laptop. "That's the newest version, isn't it?"

Clarke thinks furiously about how to ward off this unwanted interest. "Yup. My parents gave it to me as an early Christmas present. I've been complaining about how slow mine is even though I'm constantly upgrading it."

"Oh. Well, they did an excellent job picking it out. I wish I had one of those." Terry leans against the desk. "Aren't you going home for the holidays?"

"Uh, no. I was supposed to, but money is tight. I've decided to stay here. How 'bout you?" Inside, Clarke's mind is screaming to get rid of her curious coworker, but she doesn't want to raise any flags by acting weird. She's known to be a friendly, chatty person when they're not trying to meet a deadline. Her parents aren't happy she isn't returning to her hometown in Massachusetts. She does miss Swampscott, but she'd rather save her money to visit when the weather is nicer.

"Going to Maui with Troy. We leave next week. I can hardly concentrate knowing that soon we'll be lying in the sun with piña coladas in our hands." Terry gets a dreamy look on her round, youthful face.

"Sounds great. If you need help finishing any of your assignments or testing them, let me know. Can't have you stressing right before your trip." Clarke's offer to help is genuine, even if it helps to redirect Terry's attention from the new laptop.

"Thanks, Clarke. You're the best." Terry straightens up and shoots a smile Clarke's way before wandering off.

Once she leaves, Clarke refocuses on the laptop screen. Finally noticing a Haboob Software icon, Clarke clicks on the shortcut. "Oh. My. God."

Clarke looks around quickly to see whether anyone heard her outburst. She recognizes that she should be more sensitive to her surroundings right now, that she should be afraid others will somehow know her reality has changed irrevocably. Yet, all she can feel is happiness and disbelief, incredulity and joy looping through her each moment as she stares at this gift from the reputedly heartless CEO of Haboob Software.

Evidently, not so heartless.

The knowledge that this unexpected gift is from Fran sits warmly in Clarke's gut.

How is it that Fran can move her to such an extent? Time and distance seem to have no bearing—Clarke feels as drawn to Fran as the first day she met her.

And now this.

Picking up the computer quickly, Clarke strides into the restroom and enters a stall. Propping the computer on her knees, Clarke returns her attention to the computer. What she sees astounds her.

A mocked-up Christmas Special Haboob Software game, complete with graphics, audio, action choices, directions, and a special dedication that makes Clarke's insides wiggle like a dozen three-year-old's forced to sit in their chairs. "Merry Christmas to me," Clarke whispers.

Every part of the game incorporates information having to do with Clarke's life—where she lives, what she does, her education, her projects. The game has her navigating to each part of her life, earning rewards and kudos along the way. It's surprising how much Fran remembers about her. In addition, the main character is Clarke's spitting image, mole over her lip included.

Saving the dedication for last, Clarke clicks through the game, laughing at the graphics and prompted actions. They contain every project, big and small, she has ever worked on, and not only video games. She gasps when she sees the thesis project she completed for her MFA degree at the New York Film Academy. It boggles her mind to find all her collegiate, internship, and professional projects mentioned in some way within the game, including some she hasn't thought about in years. Clarke chuckles at how amateurish some of them look. She's amazed to see the improvement from the beginning of her journey to the present as it's laid out in the graphics.

After completing the game's tasks, Clarke returns to the dedication page. She pauses, dumbfounded by what she sees. It is a picture of Clarke and Fran at a company gathering. Clarke is talking to Harry while Fran gazes at Clarke tenderly, a soft smile apparent. Clarke is flabbergasted. Fran hadn't spoken more than two words to her at the event. All evidence had pointed toward Fran not caring one bit about her...but that look.

Clarke continues to study the picture. Maybe it's because she has deprived herself of really looking at Fran for so long, but she feels an unmistakable pull. Over the years, her feelings for Fran have propelled her efforts to change, to be better, to catch her attention. Perhaps Clarke's efforts were more successful than she had supposed.

Taking a deep breath, she glances one more time at the photo before focusing on the dedication.

Since leaving our illustrious company for greener pastures, Clarke Parson has quickly risen to become an impressive graphic designer and animator, digging deep to cultivate her ever-expanding knowledge and taking great risks which have paid off tenfold. Of course, we always knew how valuable, intelligent, and determined Clarke was. While in my employ, Clarke used her considerable talents to help me navigate through the myriad of endless demands on my time. I can truthfully state no one has performed as adequately. She is sorely missed.

This special game serves as a thank you to a woman who has touched many in ways she may not realize. At significant risk to her own career, Clarke stepped up to reveal valuable information when she realized someone stole our latest project from another development company. Besides saving this company millions of dollars, robbing competitors of enough ammunition to remove me from my post, and preventing Haboob Software from releasing a new game while not having the legal right to do so, Clarke has once again astounded me with her surprisingly selfless nature. I am humbled by it.

Clarke Parson is a rare, unsullied diamond. I am glad to see that life cannot scratch her beautiful surface or dim her indomitable spirit.

Clarke reads the letter several times. She is deeply touched. Shifting her attention to Fran's picture, Clarke traces her patrician features with ravenous eyes. Her signature white-haired coif, petite form, and perfect skin mesmerize her all over again. It's not so much how striking Fran looks that captivates Clarke, but rather her aura of power and her don't-fuck-with-me-ness which draws Clarke in. She guesses Fran may be about fifteen years her senior. She doesn't care. Clarke studies Fran's picture again, searching for some insight. Instead of her normal stance of looking into the camera challengingly, this photo has captured an approachable woman, someone who appreciates what she's seeing. Or someone she sees. If the photo didn't show them both, Clarke wouldn't dare believe she was the object of Fran's attention.

It is clear she will have to contact Fran to thank her. It is also clear that Fran will not punish her for doing so. It may not even be too much of a stretch to believe that Fran wants Clarke to contact her.

Hearing someone enter the bathroom, Clarke pulls toilet paper from the roll noisily, waiting for the person to enter a stall before flushing the toilet and hurrying out of the room.

Once back at her desk, Clarke places the laptop on the surface and slumps in her chair. What should she write? What Fran has done, and the time involved, boggles Clarke's mind. Staring at the dedication, she creates and discards several emails in her mind.

"Moonlighting on us, Parson?" Clarke hears. Whipping her head around, she sees Chuck Miller, a programmer, peering at her computer screen from his desk which sits kitty-corner to hers. "You know, you're supposed to work on your other projects on your own time." Clarke slams the laptop screen down as she chuckles.

"Yup. That's it exactly. You caught me. I'm sitting here while working on a project for another company, because I have no integrity and love to screw up project completion timelines." Clarke chuckles again for good measure, relaxing as Chuck joins in.

"Yeah, yeah, whatever. Now that you've saved the world, everyone is throwing the best projects at you. You're getting served filet mignon while the rest of us are eating burgers." He smirks. "Speaking of food, are you in for lunch? We're ordering Chinese."

"Sure." Clarke takes the proffered takeout menu. After he diverts his attention to the next colleague who wants to order out, Clarke opens the laptop once more. It figures that even after looking at everything while sitting on a toilet, Chuck catches her staring at the mocked-up video game. Clarke decides to give herself some slack, though. After all, this is un-Fucking-believable with a capital "F." Really.

Opening up her email, Clarke types out a message to Fran and sends it before she can talk herself out of it. As she did the last time she sent Fran an email, she keeps it simple.

Hi, again.

Merely saying thank you seems inadequate. You've always had a way of rendering me speechless. Regardless, I mean this wholeheartedly: thank you, Fran.

Clarke

Clarke wants to say so much more. She wants to tell Fran how astounded she is by the gesture she has made. She wants to admit how much she has missed Fran. She wants to ask Fran how she tracked down all the designs, animation, and storyboards Clarke has created over the years. All her collegiate and professional projects. She hadn't realized how large her portfolio has grown. She wants to convey how moved she is by this magnificent gift. However, she doubts both her ability to relate such feelings or to ask such questions. She really does feel speechless.

Purposely turning her mind toward the project that brought her into the office, Clarke shows great restraint by not looking at her email until early afternoon. Finally giving in to her desires, she refreshes her inbox and sees a response from Fran. Taking a steadying breath, Clarke opens the email.

I have recently learned that sometimes actions speak louder than words ever could. Dinner tonight? 9 o'clock at Café Pierre.

Fran

Of course Clarke agrees. Then she tries not to hyperventilate. She is going to see Fran tonight after too many years of trying to ignore the fact that she has some strong, unresolved feelings for the older woman. The only saving grace is that Fran wants to see her. *Fran. I get to call her Fran.* Only Harry gets to call her by her first name. Her body flushes as her imagination insists this is an indication that Fran misses her, too.

Not knowing how else to deal with this situation, Clarke falls back on what she has perfected. She pushes thoughts of Fran to the back of her mind and focuses on her work. Nine o'clock will come soon enough. Clarke will be able to feast her eyes and concentrate on the object of her affections.

Chapter Four

THE MEETING

ARRIVING AT THE RESTAURANT fifteen minutes early, Clarke follows the host to a table tucked in the back. She nervously rubs her sweaty hands against her black jeans and straightens out her cashmere wrap sweater, hoping Fran will like what she sees. By the time Clarke reaches the table, she feels as if she's run the New York City marathon. Clarke tingles with awareness as a piercing gaze draws her in. Fran is a welcome sight. She's dressed to kill in a black, pin-striped power suit and powder-blue silk blouse beneath. The muted lighting accentuates Fran's curves and softens the planes of her face. She is quite becoming. Stopping short to avoid walking into the host, Clarke is surprised when Fran rises to greet her.

Startling blue eyes capture Clarke's attention, holding her still as Fran slowly slides her hands down Clarke's arms. Fran pointedly peruses Clarke's body before their eyes reconnect. She nearly faints the next moment when Fran grasps Clarke's hands and leans in, kissing each cheek. Hovering near one ear, Fran says in a deep voice, "Clarke." Her voice is husky. Enticing.

Clarke tries unsuccessfully to restrain an instinctive shiver as she pulls back to look into Fran's eyes. Her pupils dilate as a slight smile graces her face. Clarke feels the urge to kiss her, even going so far as to tilt her head for a better angle. She can taste Fran's breath, a mixture of mint and coffee. At the last moment sanity kicks in and Clarke diverts her attention toward their joined hands.

Only what she sees nearly drives her crazy.

With fascination, Clarke watches as Fran slowly turns Clarke's hands, gently moving her thumbs to the base of them. Fran traces Clarke's thumbs with her own before rubbing the "v" between each thumb and forefinger. She's hypnotized as Fran strokes the inside of Clarke's hands, caressing across the middle provocatively. Clarke bites her lower lip to suppress the moan welling up.

The motions, the hands caressed so intimately, stimulate Clarke. She wishes those sensual fingers were stroking elsewhere. Feeling warmth roll through her, Clarke continues to watch the erotic thumb movements for several breathless moments. Fran is seducing her with an ease that scares Clarke.

She can feel herself losing her composure. Embracing Fran in a public setting would be suicidal. Hell, even if they were in a secluded setting, it'd still be a stupid idea. Until Clarke knows exactly what Fran wants, she intends not to act on her feelings. Although this gives finger-fucking an entirely new meaning.

Regardless, Clarke needs to stop Fran from this erotic hand-stroking before she loses control. Clarke leans toward her and whispers, "If you don't stop, I won't be held responsible for my actions." She turns her head slightly and ghosts her lips over a delicate ear, gratified when she hears a slight gasp.

"That's not much of a threat, Clarke." With one last gentle thumb stroke, Fran withdraws to rub Clarke's wrists. "As tempting as it is to spur you into action, I do not wish to be interrupted once we begin."

Fran's whispered words thrill Clarke, who cannot help but stare into alluring eyes.

"I intend to take my time." Fran releases Clarke's hands and turns to sit down. "Let's eat, Clarke. We'll need as much stamina as possible. We have years' worth of reacquainting ourselves, after all."

Clarke's eyes widen as Fran blatantly looks at her lips before once again allowing their eyes to reconnect. At Clarke's flushed face, Fran smiles devilishly. Well, that gives Clarke a fairly good idea of what Fran wants. Shaking off her arousal, Clarke dives into the deep end, needing to speak first. "Thank you, Fran. Thank you for the public endorsement and for the loaded laptop." She can feel her heart beating so hard it echoes in her ears. "You didn't have to do either. You know how your words have influenced so many in the business to contact me with job offers. And that laptop," Clarke swallows audibly, "is unbelievable. The processing speed is incredible. They will cut down on my production time and help me translate my ideas onto the screen much quicker. In fact, I'm working on a prototype for a dragon, and—" Clarke notices the soft look on Fran's face and forgets what she's saying. Luckily, the server arrives at their table.

After ordering drinks, a silence blankets them. It's not necessarily uncomfortable, but it is full. Fran reopens the conversation. "I did not expect to ever hear from you again." Clarke nods. "I am so glad to find you have not broken your habit of surprising me. I've thought about you over the years." Fran's lips curl on one side, giving her a rakish look.

"I do my best," Clarke quips. Curiosity gets the better of her. "If you thought about me, why didn't you contact me?"

"Really, Clarke. Use your pretty, little head. How could I rationalize such an action? You left me to forge your own path," Fran scoffs.

"But you wanted to," Clarke says playfully.

Fran sips her wine and glares, but her eyes shine with affection. After a loaded silence, Fran places her glass down and her stare softens once more. Clarke starts to feel a bit apprehensive. She used to be able to interpret Fran's looks. It was easy since Clarke studied Fran as often as possible. This look, however, Clarke cannot decipher.

"I had an interesting conversation with Harry just after you sent me the information on Sassy." She says the name as if she tasted something rather retch-worthy.

"Oh?" Clarke has no idea where this is going.

"I was unaware that you kept in touch. I wondered how he always knew what you were up to, the projects you were a part of."

Her gaze is so intense that Clarke's surprised Fran's eyes aren't shooting lasers. She's tempted to check the back of her head for holes. Her eyes water as she struggles not to look away. She doesn't want to miss any of the emotions swimming in those normally inscrutable eyes.

"For years now I was under the belief that you wanted nothing to do with me or my company. I received no indication that you cared at all. In fact, the way you left without looking back indicated to me your desire to leave that part of your life behind. So imagine my surprise when you swooped in to save Haboob from certain disaster."

Clarke laughs nervously. "Um, well, uh." She swallows some of her drink, stalling for time. "I couldn't allow your company to be deceived by Sig. Not once I became aware of the situation. Plus, I couldn't help but feel it was my fault. She stole the information from my computer and went to you with it, intending to trick you."

Fran waves her hand. "It wasn't your fault. She chose to steal that intellectual property. She knew what she was doing when she set out to deceive me. And she succeeded. If you hadn't acted, my company would be in quite a mess, and my job would be in jeopardy. I just can't quite figure out why you took such pains to protect me and the company when I was under the impression you wanted nothing to do with either." Fran covers Clarke's hand with her own and squeezes it before letting go. "Why, Clarke?" she asks, her voice soft.

"Just because I needed to leave doesn't mean I don't care about you. About Haboob Software—I mean Haboob Software." Clarke looks away, mortified at her slip. *Shit.* "Anyway, I did it because I could. Because she got the project details from my computer. Because she sought out your company specifically to misrepresent who has the development rights to the story." Clarke juts out her chin stubbornly. *Maybe Fran will let it go.*

"You are saying you would have taken the same action for any other company? Any other person?"

"This wouldn't have happened to anyone else. She targeted you. So, no. I acted because it was my fault that Sig sold it to you in the first place. I couldn't sit by and let it continue once I found out what she did."

"Why was I targeted?"

"I'm sure Harry told you about the connection between Sig and myself." Clarke sighs. She doesn't want to discuss how that relationship imploded. Sig's jealousy was justified, even if her actions were not.

"It's been six years since you left Haboob for better things. Why would she seek out my company to sabotage instead of one of the other companies you've worked with during those years?"

"I..." Clarke looks around the restaurant, taking in the romantic candle lighting and dimmed overhead lights, the black tablecloths and matching napkins, the full silverware setting and large, crystal wine glasses. Although this is her first time eating here, she knows it's a three-Michelin star restaurant. She sips some of the tasty pinot grigio wine, mind racing. How can she tell Fran the truth? How can she admit that Sig figured out her feelings for Fran and became the clichéd jealous lover?

Clearing her throat, Clarke exhales forcefully and shrugs. "She knew I interned with your company. Our relationship was ending, and maybe she was hoping to hurt me by hurting you, or rather, Haboob." She raises her hands in front of her and waves off the questions she can see forming. "I don't know her exact reasoning other than she knew I would never want this to happen. Please, don't ask me to explain any further. I don't know that I can." *Or that I'm willing to right now.*

Fran continues to search Clarke's eyes, hunting for the truth. Clarke valiantly holds the gaze while attempting to shield her heart. She doesn't know whether she is successful, though. In fact, she believes that, just as in the past, she cannot hide anything from this woman.

Finally, Fran offers a small smile and slight nod. "Thank you, Clarke." She looks away for a moment. "If I'd known, I—" Fran interrupts herself with a shake of the head. She looks back toward Clarke and says with a smirk, "I'll let you in on a little secret. Although I have not done so in several years, I prefer to form intimate relationships with the fairer sex, too. Now that we know we have this in common, we can move forward. Yes?"

"Yes." Clarke doesn't know how to feel about this development. What does this mean? Move forward how? This entire meal seems surreal.

After ordering their food, silence blankets them once more. Clarke has no idea what to say, how to act. "How have you been?" Clarke asks. She imagines smacking herself for such an inane question. She really does need to brush up on her conversation skills.

Fran's eyes twinkle with amusement. She delivers a full smile, transforming her face entirely. "Small talk, Clarke? Really?" Her eyes sparkle in the dim light, the shadows on her face emphasizing her defined cheekbones and strong jaw.

Clarke can do nothing but frown, provoking a chuckle from Fran. "Is it small talk if I truly want to know?" She realizes her question is ridiculous. Fran is someone who doesn't believe in social niceties, although she can charm anyone when she puts her mind to it. While an intern at Haboob, Clarke witnessed her transformation many times, charming investors and making Clarke feel so jealous of them she oftentimes had to reel herself back by thinking about her current project—anything to get her to stop wishing Fran were charming her. And yet here she is sharing a meal with Fran. This is her chance, and she's acting like a stupid schoolgirl with a crush on her favorite English teacher. Before she can really get going with her self-flagellation, Fran grasps her hand and lifts it to her lipstick-stained lips to touch as lightly as gossamer wings.

"I'm sorry, darling. Don't mind me. I recognize that this is all a bit of a shock. No doubt you haven't a clue why I invited you to dinner, much less what to say. It's been too many years since we last spoke. Too many years since I last saw you in person." She kisses Clarke's hand once more before releasing it.

Dumbfounded by Fran's words, Clarke's mouth drops open. Although not a declaration of love, anyone who knows Fran understands she never says something she doesn't mean. Hearing Fran admit it's been too long since they last talked is astounding. Amazing. On par with when Clarke earned an A from Professor Wynowski for her Marketing Video Games class. To this day, she still hates everything to do with marketing plans and data-driven reporting. Biting her lip, she gazes at Fran, who is watching her. "I agree. It has been too long." Clarke feels exposed, but she has to trust that Fran doesn't plan to hurt her.

It's not as if Fran meant to hurt her the first time. From what Clarke understands, Fran pushed her out of the nest and into freelance projects to help her on her career path. Clarke wonders whether she had other reasons. It seems impossible to believe and blasphemous to even think, but could it be possible that Fran developed feelings for her and felt it best to let her go?

Harry mentioned Fran isn't dating anyone. According to him, she lost interest after her last failed relationship. Selfishly, Clarke is glad. Her pulse speeds up as possibilities parade before her eyes like the correct numerical sequence for the lottery jackpot. Only Fran is every number Clarke needs to become rich. After trying to suppress these feelings for so long, her libido is pounding on Clarke's shoulder, impatiently demanding that Clarke listen. Is there a chance Fran may be interested in her? A chance they may explore the feelings simmering between them? A chance to figure out why Clarke felt the need to leave six years ago, and why Fran urged her to take the offered recommendation which would guarantee her steady work?

Trying to calm her nerves, Clarke sips her wine. The thought of joining Fran at her home tonight makes her feel like holding her breath, much as she did when her parents drove through a tunnel or over train tracks, anything not to blow her chance to spend time with Fran. She's afraid of saying the wrong thing, making the wrong move, or somehow calling attention to the fact that they are sitting in an exclusive restaurant sharing dinner and preparing to—what?

Does Fran really want to have sex with her? Is she willing to take such a step? Can her heart take it if all Fran wants is a casual fling?

Who is she kidding? She'll take any scraps thrown at her and kiss the woman's feet for the opportunity to touch her porcelain body and alluring lips—anything to be with this incredible woman. Clarke's attraction toward Fran began the day they met. She will not give up this chance.

Fran surprises Clarke by asking about her family. "Good. They're good. They worry about me, of course, but we talk once a week and visit every so often. I planned on going to visit them for Christmas, but I think I'll go after the holidays instead."

Clarke doesn't tell Fran about the falling out they had after she left the steady paycheck from Haboob Software. Her father was worried Clarke was throwing her life away, drifting from her friends and leaving a dream job after working hard to get it. Clarke tried to explain that Haboob Software was a stepping-stone toward a freelance career, but he was skeptical.

Once she settled into her role as an independent contractor, working on various projects as a graphic designer, things came to a head. Clarke was grieving the loss of Fran in her life even though she was making more money than while working for her. Her parents noticed. It didn't take long for them to figure out why she was so miserable. They said some unkind words, unpleasant enough that Clarke refused to interact with them for two years. When Clarke's older sister got engaged, she pleaded with Clarke to bury the hatchet. After several months of "do it for me!" Clarke relented. The reunion was uncomfortable, practically unbearable.

Over time, though, it has become easier to be in the same room. Over time, their polite inquiries have sounded less and less like the Grand Inquisition. Over time, Clarke has forgiven them for their judgmental, ignorant remarks.

Clarke idly wonders what they would say if they knew she's dining with Fran tonight, if they knew Clarke is planning to fuck this woman into next week if given the chance, if they knew that after all this time, she's still in love with this maddening, sensual, sharp-witted mystery.

She might just have to call them to share the news.

Finishing the remainder of her wine, Clarke asks, "How is Elaine?"

Fran's eyebrows rise, her face lighting up with surprise. She delivers a full smile, transforming her face entirely. "She's in her first year of college at Columbia University. Elaine has chosen to live on campus rather than to remain at home. I can't say I blame her. I miss her terribly, of course. The apartment is so quiet, so empty, without her."

Clarke can sympathize. Fran's home must resemble a mausoleum with only her in it. Not that she's ever had the privilege of visiting her home. That's probably a good thing. If she'd visited her private sanctum, she's sure she would have thrown herself at the woman. She was able to control herself in the workplace, particularly with so many colleagues around, but if they had been together in a more private setting...well, she's quite sure Fran would have fired her for indecent behavior or sexual harassment.

The air shimmers with sexual energy as they reacquaint themselves over coffee, sharing what has occurred while allowing the more intimate details to remain untouched for now. Areas exist which they're not quite ready to explore. They are feeling their way around, cautiously circling, closing the space between them with steady steps. Their conversation becomes less casual, and by the end of the meal, Clarke is confident she will be accompanying Fran home.

Eventually, the conversation dies as they gaze into one another's eyes. Clarke is a glutton, greedily staring at Fran, not able to get her fill. The look in Fran's eyes causes a spike of arousal to course through her. Clarke watches, enthralled, as Fran tilts her head and says, "Come home with me, Clarke."

And it's as simple as that.

Clarke's response is a wolfish smile. No reason not to let her desire shine through now. Fran's eyes glow as she reads Clarke's body language. It clearly states how Clarke can't wait to get her hands on Fran. Remarkably, it seems Fran feels the same way.

Chapter Five

ACTIONS SPEAK LOUDER THAN WORDS

THEY DO NOT TALK during the ride to Fran's home. They do not kiss, although Clarke is nearly desperate to feel those lips against hers. They fall into silence, reminiscent of times they sat together at Haboob, working on their computers for hours at a time. It is comfortable, soothing, familiar.

All those feelings transform into rising arousal when Fran's fingers begin to trace patterns on Clarke's thigh. Staring at the competent fingers creating circles and ovals, spirals and figure eights, Clarke nearly goes mad with the desire to pull Fran into a crushing hug before mapping her enticing contours with an eager mouth. She doesn't dare move an inch.

The interior of the vehicle feels like those few moments before storm clouds release their burden, and Clarke feels like an unprepared child staring at those clouds in awe. Clarke isn't sure she's ready for what happens next, yet she's excited to find out. She does know not to do anything as stupid as stopping Fran's finger-play. Instead, she focuses on her breathing as Fran becomes bolder. Her fingers ring Clarke's kneecap before converging on the tip and pushing out forcefully in all directions. Clarke never realized what an erogenous zone the knee can be. Maybe it's just Fran's hand which creates that reaction, regardless of where she touches. Her fingers climb to Clarke's hip, hypnotic caresses gliding up and down her thigh before zigzagging in wide arcs and ending where Clarke's panty line rests. Clarke is weak with want.

On shaky legs she follows Fran inside her modern apartment and up the stairs, straight into the master suite. She's disappointed to not have time to study any part of the apartment since the lights are off. She consoles herself by keeping her eyes on Fran, appreciating the way she moves. Once Clarke crosses the room's threshold, she stops, fascinated to see hunger reflected in bright eyes as Fran sweeps them from head to foot. Without a word, she glides over to Clarke and removes her coat. She trembles when Fran removes it from her shoulders and trails her fingers down Clarke's shoulder blades. With a gentle hand on Clarke's lower back, Fran guides her to the four-poster, king-sized bed and stops next to it.

The bed is beautiful. It's covered with a navy-print comforter and matching silk pillows, a throw on the bottom of the bed ready for the cooler nights. The bed shows that Fran doesn't skimp on high-quality bedding. Clarke wants to wander around the room and discover all Fran's secrets, but that will have to wait. This night isn't meant for Clarke to spend learning about Fran's life. It's meant for her to spend learning about Fran's body, as Fran learns hers. Clarke is sure she will die before she's able to explore anything if Fran doesn't touch her soon. That would be a damn shame. Fran steps in her space, and Clarke thanks a god she doesn't believe in as she looks into smoldering eyes.

As if to memorize it, Fran runs delicate fingers over Clarke's face. "I've missed your face." Fran's whispered words fill Clarke with amazement. Fran frames Clarke's face with her hands and brushes her lips against Clarke's mouth gently. "Your smile." Fran nibbles Clarke's lower lip for several wonderful moments, and Clarke doesn't hold back the needy moan that wells up from her soul. "Those expressive chocolate eyes," Fran says as she kisses Clarke's neck. "And, although it didn't quite hit me fully until I saw you tonight," Fran says while gazing into Clarke's eyes. "I've missed *you*." Returning to Clarke's waiting lips, Fran delivers more kisses, each one more profound, each one communicating a rich yearning to be closer.

Clarke wonders whether all those years of denying her feelings combined with her knowledge that Fran could never, ever return her love, have thrown her into some type of psychotic break. Certainly, she is not kissing Fran Silvetti, the woman she has loved from afar for so, so long. It is not possible. Any moment now she will return to her lonely reality, crying over her stupid heart and foolish dreams. Any moment now.

A tongue seeking entrance causes Clarke to moan loudly. She practically swoons as Fran takes her time, exploring the contours of her mouth before stroking their tongues together gloriously. Clarke realizes that Fran has bent her backward, practically prostrate on the bed, while holding her head steady. Clarke's body burns with need, thanks to Fran's single-minded focus on plundering her mouth. She's sure she'll combust from disbelief, heat, ecstasy, or some combination.

When Fran finally ends the kiss, she does not release Clarke's face. They stare at each other. Panting lightly, not knowing what will happen next, Clarke's enthralled by Fran's passion-darkened eyes and flushed face. This is so outside of her imagination, she can do nothing but wait for Fran to say something, do something.

Moving her hands to Clarke's upper arms, Fran pulls her into an upright position. Their bodies become flush, and Clarke loses what little breath she has regained. Fran smirks as she wraps her arms around Clarke's waist, holding her close. Clarke would feel embarrassed, but when she runs reverent hands over Fran's shoulder blades, she feels her tremble. Satisfaction blazes through Clarke.

Fran wasn't exaggerating when she proclaimed she wished to take her time. She takes pains to remove each piece of Clarke's clothing separately, kissing the revealed skin with a reverence which leaves Clarke breathless. By the time Fran allows Clarke to sink on the bed, she has kissed every inch of Clarke's torso, arms, hands, neck, and face. Once she's on the bed, Fran continues her reverent kisses on her legs and toes. She lies exposed and wanting as Fran delivers these tender kisses. Clarke's body thrums with desire even as she struggles not to pass out from the sheer pleasure she is experiencing. She shudders as Fran's humid mouth sucks on her ear, nibbling teasingly before pulling away to remove her own clothing.

If Clarke thought she might pass out while Fran was undressing her, that is nothing compared to how she feels as she watches Fran disrobe. She removes her suit jacket, revealing a sleeveless shell tucked in to tailored pinstripe slacks which showcase her curves. This is a woman, hips shifting as she allows her slacks to pool at her feet. She steps out of shoes and pants together, and Clarke's eyes devour toned, porcelain legs from dainty feet to the hem of her silk blouse. Clarke whimpers as Fran removes her top, revealing matching bra and panties. She notes with distraction how the navy set matches the bedspread. Her fingers tingle with the desire to remove the lingerie, but Fran does so without delay and only waits long enough for Clarke's eyes to glide across every inch revealed. As Fran prowls toward Clarke, she wonders whether she'll survive this encounter. After years of fantasizing, she realizes she never could have anticipated the passion erupting between them.

Fran climbs up Clarke's body, bracketing her with knees and elbows as she returns to Clarke's lips and kisses her. What starts as the soft brushing of lips grows into long, luscious kisses, slowly building like a wonderful song full of sweet woodwinds, romantic violins, passionate horns, and pulsating percussion. Fran's tongue strokes hers with all-encompassing swipes that fulfill Clarke in ways she has never experienced. As she surrenders to this lovemaking, allowing Fran to explore and possess, she feels Fran's fingers slide into her, pushing and withdrawing in much the same motion she demonstrated while holding Clarke's hands in the restaurant.

Clarke doesn't last long. The passion is too hot, the urgency too compelling. When Fran commands her to let go, to not hold back, it doesn't enter her mind to do anything other than comply. She might feel embarrassed if she had any brain cells left to fire the mortification synapses into action. Instead, she screams Fran's name into the night, tucking her head into her neck as her body convulses in ecstasy. It is possible she blacks out for a few moments.

When she begins to pull together her spectacularly shattered composure, she feels Fran's fingers, those miraculous digits, gently combing through her damp curls over and over. A bubble of happiness swells within Clarke's chest as she enjoys the tender caresses. Fran's actions seem totally against her persona. Clarke feels privileged to receive such special treatment, to be able to enjoy a side of Fran she never knew existed.

Sighing, Clarke kisses Fran's collarbone and lifts her head to look in her eyes. They are open to her, expressing affection and desire. Now that she has recovered, Clarke sets out to love this woman just as thoroughly, just as reverently, just as passionately.

Turning Fran so she is supine on the bed, Clarke delivers soft kisses to her eyelids, her nose, her forehead, her chin, to that stubborn jaw and to those defined cheeks. "I tried to forget your face," Clarke mutters. Moving to one side, Clarke kisses around the ear, humming her approval when Fran accommodatingly angles her head to provide better access. "I tried to forget how much you mean to me." Sucking on an earlobe, Clarke hears Fran's groan. It encourages her to continue with explorations behind the ears and a long, unhurried journey down her neck. "But I couldn't. No amount of discipline could keep you out of my dreams." Clarke can hardly believe she's confessing these truths, but she feels confident Fran won't reject her. Not here. Not now.

Although she would be content to continue in this vein all night, she sees the erratic pulse jumping in Fran's neck and feels hands tightening around her head as sensual hips gyrate against her body. Slithering down Fran's torso, Clarke begins to pay attention to gorgeous breasts. Palming them, weighing them, worshiping them with her fingers, lips, and tongue, Clarke nips and sucks, pinches, and pulls as she listens to Fran's responses become increasingly vocal. "Clarke," and "oh," and "mmmm" punctuate Fran's whimpers and mewls, driving Clarke to suck on one erect nub while pulling on the other one. Soon, Fran's pants give way to a shriek as her body stiffens. She flops back, her body boneless, as she pants. Clarke doesn't feel so mortified now.

They cling together as Fran takes deep breaths. "Clarke," Fran whispers, as she holds her in a tight embrace. Although the room is cool, they're both sweating, the heat created through their lovemaking keeping them warm. Clarke's mind is blissfully blank, her ear over the steady heartbeats under her. As it slows to a resting rhythm, Clarke focuses on fingers running up and down her spine.

Not sure what Fran wants, Clarke remains quiet while wrapped in her arms, waiting for some indication. It is possible she sleeps for a bit. When Clarke opens her eyes, she latches onto bright-blue eyes. "Hey." Clarke's whisper is more of a confirmation she's awake than a conversation opener.

Fran smiles and pulls Clarke closer to kiss. "You are a gift, Clarke. In fact, today is my birthday, and I have wished to hold you in this way for many years." Fran's words stun her. All she can think to do is to lean in for another kiss.

This time their lovemaking is slow, as if they have the rest of their lives. Clarke makes a leisurely and thorough investigation of Fran's body leisurely, enchanted by Fran's reactions to her touch. Their motions reflect a deepness, a presence that enfolds Clarke's heart. She thinks about how long she has desired Fran, how hopeless it all seemed, how thankful she is for this chance to express herself in this way to a woman who has haunted her dreams since the moment their paths first crossed. She's carried a torch for a long time. How unexpected it is to find it has lit the way to Fran's bed.

Sliding over peaks and valleys with her mouth, she stalls at Fran's weeping center. Clarke licks delicately around the clitoris and downward to suck the labia. Wiggling her tongue at Fran's entrance, she feels hands gently pushing her face away. Confused, Clarke looks up at the extremely aroused woman.

"Come here and turn around. I want to taste you." Clarke's always been good at following Fran's directions, and she has no intention of disappointing her now. Fran guides her back into her arms and delivers a forceful kiss that skyrockets Clarke's desire. She turns around and hovers over Fran's body while her feet are facing the headboard. As she returns her lips to Fran's center, she's mindful not to place her entire weight on her. Exploring Fran with her tongue and lips once more, she nearly jumps out of her skin when she feels hands on her hips and a tongue dipping inside her.

Moaning Fran's name, Clarke undulates, knees on either side of Fran's head. It feels so good. She wants to sink her hips downward, to impale herself on that wicked tongue. After a few moments, Clarke begins to rock in time with Fran's motions. She nearly comes when Fran grasps her ass and pulls her down firmly, nipping at her clitoris and swirling her tongue around it. She squeaks, her motions becoming more frenetic, as she begins to lick more forcefully at Fran's nerve center, determined for them to climax together. Fran's breathy groans, signifying her impending orgasm, shoot straight through Clarke, and she can no longer control her body. As their shouts commingle, Clarke feels her body spasm for long moments, days, centuries. Pleasure washes through her relentlessly. Quivering so much she fears she will collapse on Fran. Clarke laps up the flow of moisture from her center while leaning on shaky elbows and knees.

After resting her head on Fran's inner thigh for a few minutes Clarke lifts her sated body up to resettle next to Fran, her head still pointed toward the end of the bed. Clarke doesn't yet have the strength to rejoin her. Fran slowly strokes Clarke's leg as they rest. Feeling sleepy, Clarke crawls up the bed and settles next to Fran, who turns to deliver a lingering kiss. Soon they both fall into a deep, satisfied sleep.

When Clarke wakes, she can tell it is early the next morning. She can hear the pitter-patter of rain on the windowpanes. She closes her eyes, words running through her head.

Figures on the bedroom shade
Imprints by the rain
Incantations made by the primal dance
Of two lovers
Tangled
In the same dream

She hopes this will happen again. She wants her body tangled with Fran's. She wants to hear the sounds she makes and feel their bodies move together. Opening her eyes, Clarke props her head on her arm and studies the sleeping woman. How she loves her. If she harbored any doubt, if she maintained any illusion that her fantasies were merely the work of wanting the unattainable, last night clarified her feelings dramatically. She had missed Fran's caustic wit, razor-sharp intellect, and powerful presence. More than that, the thought of never feeling those hands on her body again, of never tasting those lips or hearing that voice call out to her as ecstasy overtakes her, causes panic to rise within Clarke.

Fran chooses that moment to open her eyes. Perhaps she sees how unsure Clarke feels, perhaps she recognizes Clarke's need, or perhaps she understands a real chance exists that this will be their only night together. Whatever it is that stirs Fran to surge forward and pin Clarke to the bed as she plunders Clarke's mouth with ruthless abandon, Clarke can feel the desperation oozing through her and it comforts her. She isn't the only one fighting to make this last, wanting more than one night can offer.

Wrapped firmly in Fran's arms much later, Clarke hears Fran whisper, "I do not wish to watch you walk away again." Clarke kisses Fran's breastbone and settles into her body as if she plans to hibernate for the foreseeable future.

Clarke isn't sure how to respond. Never in a million years would she have believed Fran might desire her, might want Clarke in her life. She is afraid to say something too over the top, too revealing, something that may invite sarcasm or rejection. Before she drops off to sleep Clarke murmurs, "I'm right here. Happy birthday, Fran." She feels the reactionary tightening of arms around her in reply and knows this is where she always wants to be.

Chapter Six

ANOTHER MEETING

BY THE TIME CLARKE wakes, the spot beside her is cold. Although the curtains are drawn, the morning light seeps through the edges, illuminating the room enough for Clarke to know she's slept longer than she should have. In the early morning light, she gets her first good look at Fran's bedroom. It's beautiful. Calm. Comfortable. The color scheme is a warm eggshell color with matching floral drapes and a rich brown Berber rug. A seating area near the windows seems to invite her to read the paper and gaze at the Hudson River, and she spies a door that opens to a small balcony. She hopes she'll have the opportunity to gaze at the river from the balcony in the future.

Looking at the time on her cell phone, Clarke leans over the side of the bed, searching for her clothes. She doesn't have much time to get home, change, and get to work. They only have two more weeks before releasing the game, and she has several tweaks to finish, not to mention the social media platforms to update. After pulling on her panties and jeans while remaining stretched out on the bed, she sits up to scour the floor with her eyes for her bra and sweater. She supposes turning on the light would prove helpful, yet she hesitates to do anything that might bring attention to herself. It's ridiculous. She isn't a thief searching for loot or an uninvited guest. *Then why do I feel like this?*

Shaking her head, Clarke grabs her cellphone and turns on the flashlight. She finds the rest of her clothes farther away from the bed and rises to grab them. After she finishes dressing, she decides to take another minute to look around the room before she leaves. *This might be my only chance*, she thinks, sadness welling within her. Pushing those feelings aside, she moves away from the unmade bed.

A beautiful wooden armoire against the far wall matches the bedside tables and a small bookshelf. She itches to explore the books, but she feels that might be invasive. She gazes at the gas fireplace and fervently wishes she'd felt its heat on her nude form last night while they made love. Fran has always been able to read Clarke like an open book, and the previous night proved to be no exception. She shivers, remembering how Fran touched her.

Noticing a few framed photos, Clarke moves close enough with the light to recognize they're of Fran's daughter at various ages, some with her, and others at different events over the years. Elaine has blossomed into a lovely young woman. It doesn't escape her that she's closer to Elaine's age than Fran's age. The age gap doesn't matter one whit to Clarke. After last night Clarke can't imagine being with anyone else. She takes one final look around the spacious room before walking through the open door.

Light streams through windows across from the staircase and the second-floor rooms. Walking down the hallway, she sees another bedroom, a spacious bathroom, and a home office. She's disappointed to find all the rooms empty. She's tempted to freshen up in the bathroom, but she'd rather continue with trying to find Fran. She retraces her steps, stalling at the top of the stairs. An alcove offers a seating area arranged in front of another small bookcase with some videogame magazines splayed on top.

Clarke descends the stairs, stopping at the landing where a window seat reveals the same view as in Fran's room. It looks like the perfect place to sit to contemplate life. She turns to look down the rest of the stairs and with reluctance makes her way to the entryway. She listens for any indication Fran is puttering around somewhere on the first floor, but it's in vain. She can find her nowhere.

It would have been nice if Fran had at least left a note or something. Clarke feels a bit cheap, a bit used, and very confused. She had gotten the distinct impression that last night would not be a one-night stand, but now she's not so sure. She wonders whether Fran's final words meant she did not intend to be present when Clarke left her home. Clarke shakes her head. She doesn't understand. Not willing to explore any more of the apartment, Clarke leaves, slamming the door on her way out. She knows it's juvenile, but it's not like anyone is home to hear it.

Although Clarke doesn't arrive at Runaway Games until well after nine in the morning, no one mentions it. That's one of the perks of being a contract worker. She makes her own hours. Still, she likes to be professional, and she feels bad that she's tardy. She sets up her laptop and video screens, determined to ignore her confusion and anger for how she awoke. She promises herself she isn't reverting to her tried-and-true default of ignoring what happened the night before or her unflagging feelings for Fran.

That's not what this is. She simply can't afford to moon over Fran when she has so much to do. Now is not the time. She can brood and rehash and examine every moment of last night, beginning with her arrival at Café Pierre and ending at Fran's home once she finishes her workday.

After a rushed morning, Clarke leans back in her chair and exhales loudly. While awaiting feedback on the latest changes she made to *End of the World, the Greenhouse Effect*, she's been attempting to finish the animation for a new fantasy project. Her dragons aren't moving naturally. Maybe her heart isn't in it. Apparently, it has remained in an apartment uptown. Clarke refuses to think about what happened. Not here. Not now. She needs to focus on her work. Later, when she is alone in her cold, cold bed, she can relive those hours. She's successfully pushed those thoughts aside all day. A few more hours should be a piece of cake.

When her phone rings, Clarke eyes it curiously. "Clarke here." She saves her work and stares sightlessly at the dragon frozen on the screen. People are talking in low murmurs throughout the room, most staring at the screens in front of them. She can see Dirk pointing at one screen as he talks, the two programmers nodding at what he's saying. They have a team meeting in forty-five minutes to update him on where everyone is with their assignments. Clarke's hoping to get feedback on her assignments before the meeting.

"Delivery up front for ya." A feeling of déjà vu steals over her when she hears the words.

"Thanks." Clarke strides to the front while wondering what it can be. Her entire life changed from yesterday's delivery. Unfortunately, it's too early to tell if the change is positive. She supposes that will depend on whether she ever hears from Fran again. Maybe last night was a thank-you-for-saving-my-ass fuck. And what an ass it is. Or maybe it was a proper goodbye, one they should have shared six years ago.

When she reaches the front desk, Clarke's eyes fill with tears of relief. Waiting for her is a stunning bouquet of roses and an envelope. Thanking the receptionist, Clarke returns to her workspace while thoughts swirl through her mind. Obviously, these are from Fran. Excitement flows through her with the realization that Fran may want to see her again. That feeling vies with her righteous anger. She's not impressed that Fran left her alone in an empty house after their first night together. *But these roses are impressive*, a little voice whispers in her mind. She wonders whether she should throw them in the trash and move on. She doesn't want to be the girl who allows her partner to treat her like she's not worth any effort, waiting for any positive sign and accepting it with a smile. *As if I'm strong enough to turn away from her after knowing how she tastes.*

Before opening the envelope, she takes the time to appreciate the tastefully arranged bouquet of coral roses ringed with red, offset with greenery. The attached envelope, heavy gilded stock of the whitest ivory, reflects elegance, sophistication, and wealth. On the front is her name. She can't help but smile as she recognizes the methodical handwriting. So in control. Nothing like last night.

Sliding the stationery from the enclosure, Clarke's nostrils flare as she catches the slightest hint of Fran's perfume. That fragrance has imprinted itself on her soul, along with many other sensory triggers from last night.

Clarke,

I owe you breakfast. Saturday at the Ritz, 10:00 a.m.?
F.

Although her first inclination is to agree, Clarke cannot help but wonder why Fran left without a word. *Why is she sending flowers and an invitation? What does she want? For that matter, what do I want?*

Weariness settles over her like a heavy blanket in the middle of a heatwave. It smothers her, makes it hard for her to breathe. Not knowing how Fran feels, her motivation for contacting her again is perplexing. Clarke doesn't know whether seeing her again is a good idea. She hangs her head in defeat. Her need outranks any logical thoughts she has of protecting her heart by walking away. If she has the chance to hold Fran again, she'll take it.

Although she can't speak for Fran or what she wants, Clarke knows she wants it all. She wants to spend time with Fran. She wants to make love with her. She wants to be able to call her when she misses her, and she wants Fran to call her. For now, though, she is content with messengers and formal invitations. Fran's actions reassure her that she wants something, too. With that thought in mind, Clarke sends an email accepting the invitation. She ignores her misgivings. She ignores her hurt feelings. She ignores everything except her elation that Fran wants to see her again. She hangs on to the certainty that Fran does not equivocate or mince words. If she did not want to spend more time with Clarke, she wouldn't invite her to breakfast.

After the team meeting, Clarke spends the rest of the day immersed in social media and website updates. She sees the number of website visitors has increased since yesterday. Her goal is to keep increasing the clicks by updating all the platforms twice a day—late morning and before she leaves for the evening. She has an approved plan of what to post. The first posting each day focuses on a character, highlighting their talents, occupation, hometown, and astrology sign. The team has pitched in with ideas, and it doesn't take much time to write up the descriptions since she tends to create a background story for each character she creates. It helps her build in quirks and unique qualities. She posts different images on each social media website and a short animation on Runaway Games' website. She knows Haboob is doing something similar.

Today Twitter is going crazy with comments and retweets. People are getting psyched for the release of the game, trying to get an invite to the launch party. Clarke is giving away twenty-five sets of tickets between now and the launch. She's loading a new video on Tiktok and YouTube with some behind-the-scenes graphics and background on the game's narrative. Next week, she'll livestream playing the first level on Discord. She's looking forward to people's reactions as she shows some of the Easter eggs they've placed in the game. If she's feeling generous, she might even reveal the secret path that helps them bypass wading through a river filled with toxic dye waste dumped by the textile factory. It seems as if the world has revealed an Easter egg for her to explore in the image of Fran Silvetti. Clarke is looking forward to discovering what comes next.

***

Clarke arrives at the Ritz before Fran, and the hostess shows her to a table overlooking Central Park. She's nervous. She doesn't know what to expect. Is Fran going to let her down easy? Tell her that their night together was enjoyable but will not happen aain? The thought is unbearable. Getting to experience Fran in that way was a revelation. As she has for the previous couple of days, Clarke talks herself off the ledge. She knows Fran wouldn't invite her to breakfast if she doesn't want any more personal interactions with her.

"Clarke."

Clarke looks up so quickly she feels a twinge in her neck. Fran bends toward her to deliver a lingering kiss on the cheek, a thumb briefly brushing the other one. Clarke draws in a shaky breath as she watches Fran seat herself, a pensive expression on her face. She's dressed in casual black slacks and a fir-green corded sweater. She looks warm and relaxed. She wears minimal makeup, only enough to bring attention to her eyes and lips. Clarke takes the opportunity to soak in the sight, not knowing whether this is the final time she'll have Fran's undivided attention. She bites her lower lip hard, chastising herself for allowing her fears to get the better of her. It seems all the pep talks in the world can't push aside her insecurities.

"How are you, Clarke?" Fran asks, after a soul-searching gaze, her voice soft.

Clarke doesn't know how to answer. She wants to tell Fran that she is confused and bewildered. That she wants to spend more time with her. That she doesn't understand why she woke up alone after a night which changed her life. That she's angry and hurt, but all those feelings have taken a backseat to her elation at seeing her again. "Fine."

Fran studies her for a moment. "Hmm. I can see that."

It's possible Fran understands 'fine' equals 'I am so beyond confused.' Knowing how she can never hide her emotions, it's possible Fran can interpret what she's feeling with one look at her expression. Clarke clasps her hands together on top of her lap and stares out the window. It's a pretty view. She remains silent, unsure what to say or how to act. She concentrates on keeping her breathing even and face inscrutable. She doubts she's fooling Fran for a second.

They order their food and Clarke goes back to staring outside. People hurry down the street, the blustery wind a deterrent to those who might wish to spend an extended amount of time outdoors. Regardless of the relentless gusts, people flood the streets, many carrying bags full of holiday gifts. Although she cannot hear them, she notes many small groups conversing and laughing as they head toward their next destination. She takes out a small pad and draws a few people in various poses, thinking she can use them in future games. She grins at the little girl with the matching winterwear, topped off with a large pompom on her red hat. She skips down the street, holding on to her mom's hand. It reminds her of days long past when each day closer to Christmas ratcheted up her excitement.

Fran doesn't interrupt or seem to mind. She sips her coffee while watching Clarke draw. Sig always hated when Clarke did this, insisting she put the pad away and pay attention to her. She always liked being the center of attention. Clarke supposes that hasn't changed. She received an angry voicemail after blowing the whistle on her duplicitousness. It incriminated her even more, and Clarke was happy to forward it to Fran and Dirk. She doesn't know whether they'll be pressing charges against Sig, but either way, Clarke's happy to forward as much evidence as she can find to make sure Sig doesn't get away with doing this to anyone else.

Although their breakfast is a silent affair, Clarke begins to relax. She is content to be in Fran's company, even if Fran isn't allaying her fears or answering her unasked questions. Fran is taking time out of her day to be with her. That must be enough.

As their server clears their table of plates Fran asks, "Are you working today?"

"At three," Clarke says. The calmness she felt throughout their breakfast falls away as her senses sharpen. She tries to keep herself from getting excited, from jumping to conclusions. Even though she hopes Fran wants to spend more time with her, she won't assume. She can't. Fran's hand on hers signals she should pay attention.

"I'm sorry I wasn't home when you woke up. I wasn't trying to hurt your feelings or indicate you're not important. Nothing is further from the truth."

Clarke watches Fran's thumb rubbing her wrist, her mind swirling. She's never heard Fran apologize for anything, but maybe she only offers them for personal matters. She wants to ask questions. She wants to clear the air. She wants to expel her anger, and confusion, and dismay. She also wants to move on from these uncomfortable feelings and the fear of how Fran may react if she expresses herself. She swallows thickly, clearing her throat and sniffing. Her eyes burn with repressed emotions. She feels her hand squeezed and looks up.

"Come home with me, Clarke?" Fran's eyes are shimmering with promises, head tilted in that way Clarke loves.

She feels relief roar through her as she nods her head. *As if there's any doubt. I'd follow her anywhere.*

Before utilizing the privacy partition, Fran directs her driver to pick them up from the apartment at 2:00 p.m. Once settled in the back of the car, Fran turns to Clarke and intertwines their fingers. A moment later Fran is kissing Clarke, and she feels herself melt. She fervently hopes this will not be the last time. This just can't be, because Clarke is realizing she must have the privilege of kissing these lips for the rest of her life. She must be able to feel her lips and taste her breath and swallow her moans. Fran must allow her to explore every inch of her strong chin and dainty ears, her lovely collarbones and defined shoulder blades. She needs to taste and touch, search and discover what causes Fran to gasp and mewl and moan and whimper. She needs to know because such knowledge will keep her warm on those cold nights when they aren't together. It will keep her going after Fran grows tired of her and sets her free once again. She needs to store up these moments and commit them to memory so that when she no longer receives this magnificent woman's love, she'll be able to relive these moments and know that for a time, Fran wanted her—a woman she paid scant attention to when they worked together.

When the car stops, Fran pulls away and Clarke mourns the loss of her warm body and addictive lips. Fran murmurs, "Clarke," as she trails a thumb down her cheek, and Clarke's fears burn away under her warm gaze. She isn't being set free today, and to Clarke, that's all she cares about. For today, her heart will remain intact. And it's as simple as that.

Chapter Seven

WORKING OUT THE KINKS

ARRIVING AT THE LAUNCH party twenty minutes before it opens to the public, Fran walks through the venue, mentally checking off what state each station is in—finished, in process, or not yet started. The devil is in the details, and she wants to work out any unforeseen hiccups before any guests arrive. They rented out an eco-friendly venue that boasts energy-efficient lighting, low-flow water fixtures, a solid waste diversion partnership, and donations of used toiletries, sterilized and distributed to people in need. It also has a green wall on the building façade and a green roof with an irrigation system they use to collect rainwater. If it weren't so cold, they would have used the roof for part of the exhibition. Although only the beginning of November, the nights dip into the low thirties.

She stands near the entrance to the conference hall and allows her eyes to scan the area, trying to see it through the eyes of a guest. Directly inside on the right are three long tables for automated registration. They only need to enter their names and email addresses. Once registered, they will receive an email with a ninety-day free subscription to the game, as well as a code to download it. That way they can play alone or play online with others. As guests wander about, they'll see booths set up with different eco-friendly themes, such as how to lessen the effects of powerplants, transportation, deforestation, fossil fuels, and waste. It's not all-inclusive, and they've tried to make sure their displays are engaging and not preachy. The last thing she wants to do is get into an ideological debate.

Next to the booths is a side room decorated with beautiful plants of assorted sizes. They'll have the game's music playing in the background and a game demo playing on a loop which introduces the main characters and their quests. They're using many of the demos Clarke has introduced through social media and their websites. Fran feels a pleasant fluttering in her belly at the thought of seeing Clarke.

Hired actors will circulate around the room, dressed as various characters for photo opportunities. In keeping with the eco-friendly theme, the snacks and drinks they'll offer are both from companies which give back to communities and from Earth-friendly organizations. She firmly vetoed the idea of only offering vegetarian, or even more restrictive, a vegan selection of finger foods. This is still a party, and she prefers to offer a wide variety of snacks.

On the far side of the room is a large area set up for guests to try the game, and they can sign up for matches which will occur throughout the evening. Winners shall advance throughout the night, eventually paired to semifinal and final matches. Those winners will receive a year of online streaming not only for this game but for other Haboob Software games, too. Those who make it to the semifinals will receive online gaming for a selection of Runaway Games. All games are accessible on Discord and both companies' websites.

To Fran's left are tables which will hold gifts for all attendees. Bright Gerbera Daisy plants in biodegradable pots cover several tables, their red, orange, yellow, pink, and white hues brightening the area. On separate tables are rolls of bamboo toilet paper, beach towels made from recycled plastic, and water bottles made of hemp, all with the game logo and graphics. They have several different types of small swag items at the various booths, each eco-friendly and geared to emphasize a part of the game. Although this game has less-than-altruistic storylines and choices which may yield successful outcomes, she's also proud it promotes making the harder, necessary options to save Earth. Clarke did an excellent job with creating backstories for some of the main characters and game goals. Haboob was able to incorporate nearly all the work Clarke completed on the project before she contacted Fran to reveal Sig's deception.

Fran couldn't say the same for much of the programming created by Runaway Games' employees. Dirk wasn't happy with that pronouncement, but as Fran pointed out, at the end of the day, Runaway Games was going to earn a pretty profit, much bigger than what they originally expected. So all shall end well, and Dirk's ego has been stroked into submission. Wrinkling her nose at the thought, she looks around restlessly, wondering when Clarke will arrive.

A shiver runs down Fran's spine at the thought of seeing her again. It really has been too long. She hasn't allowed herself the luxury of thinking about the beguiling woman since they shared breakfast at the Ritz and a lovely interlude before returning to work. She's held Clarke in her arms and made love to her on two occasions, and if she has her way, she will hold her again tonight. It confounds her, knowing she wasted six years—years she could have shared with Clarke. Fran thought she was doing what was best for her, but now she wonders whether she pushed Clarke out the door in a misguided attempt to protect her own heart.

People walk in and out of the large room, the constant cacophony creating a comfortable backdrop to her racing thoughts. She can see the event coming together, feel the buoyant mood infusing the space. So much work goes into a launch, yet not having one is unthinkable. It will be livestreamed on several platforms, introducing the game to those not able to attend, even awarding several game codes to those watching the event through their devices.

Hearing Clarke's voice, she peers over her shoulder and watches her juggling computer equipment and her cell phone while walking toward the far side of the room. Clarke's eyebrows are low over her eyes, her cheeks flushed, and her voice sharp. Fran has never witnessed Clarke's anger, never heard her voice slice through the air like a hot knife through butter. She felt protectiveness roar through her. Someone is hurting Clarke. Someone is dimming her light. Fran steps forward to follow Clarke, but she's stopped by Harry.

"Ready to be overrun by the mob? There's a line around the corner." He rubs his hands together. "This is going to be an incredible launch. I can feel it."

Fran takes a good look at her right-hand man. He's pulled back his long, black hair into a man-bun. His dark mustache and beard have grown enough to make him appear like a rugged, dangerous guy—in keeping with a Celtic warrior in one of their video games. Girls tend to flock to him like flies, and although she wouldn't label him as a heartbreaker, he hasn't met anyone who's kept his interest for long. He's wearing a dark-green tweed vest over a black, button-down shirt and matching black jeans. He'll have no problem finding companionship tonight if he's on the prowl.

"I agree. I have no doubt this will give us the boost we need to top the list of holiday gifts, even as we educate gamers on Earth's fate if we don't start taking care of it." Her eyes catch sight of a lackey sitting on a table, chatting with a pretty girl while several boxes remain unpacked. This will not do. "Excuse me while I educate one of our soon-to-be-ex employees about why he is no longer employed." Before she can take two steps, Harry stops her with a hand on her arm.

"Let me take care of Romeo. No need for unpleasantness until after the launch. We need good juju and all that." He pulls down on his vest in an amusing version of Captain Picard, adopts a stern expression, and strides away.

Fran watches him hurry over to the drone before turning away to search for Clarke. Of course, with so many people and the space between them, it is a fool's errand. Although she has the urge to find her, she knows how irregular that would seem. No, she'll have to find her later, perhaps once the final competitions take place. She knows Clarke will be coordinating the games and remaining on hand to answer any questions. She'll also provide insider tips about how to advance to the next levels.

"May I have everyone's attention?" Harry stands in the middle of the cavernous room, arms waving over his head, hooked up to a mic. "Great. Thank you for all your hard work to get us ready for the launch. Many of you worked on the game in some capacity, so I know you feel as much pride as I do with the product we've created. Doors will open in five minutes, so please make sure you're ready for the masses. If you need help, we have people wearing red shirts—raise your hands red-shirt people—who have walkie-talkies and will let us know to send someone over right away. Any questions?"

No one says anything, and Fran is glad to see everyone looks alert and ready. Most employees have participated in at least one launch in the past. She knows this is true since she approved the roster list for every person here tonight. Several of the Brightman-Cook board members will be in attendance, and she doesn't want any hiccups with the event. She knows the night will be successful—if not, heads will roll.

Harry calls names from his list, making sure each person knows where to be. "Okay." Harry claps his hands. "Two-minute warning, friends. Get your game faces on."

In some pockets of the room, titters erupt—probably more obligatory than due to their believing Harry's little pun is funny. He paces toward the back, and Fran pushes down the bolt of jealousy she feels. She knows he's going to talk to Clarke. She also knows she will see that woman in all her wondrous glory in a mere few hours. That reminder keeps her calm, and she focuses on the present moment.

The doors open, and the noise volume increases to a happy hum as people register. Oh yes, this night will be phenomenal. In so many ways. Fran turns to the person who appears at her elbow, ready to play her part. She knows the next few hours will pass in the blink of an eye.

"Hey there, pretty lady." Eyebrow hiking up, Fran turns to find Clarke smiling at her. She's probably the only person on Earth with the chutzpah to call her that.

"Idle on launch night?" Fran asks.

"No way. I'm rounding up people to play the game." Clarke holds a clipboard, which she has filled with names.

"Yes, well, don't let me keep you. I'll see you after—" Fran is interrupted by a smarmy voice she knows all too well.

"Hello, Fran. You must be happy with how many people are here. And who's this? A new intern? You certainly attract the prettiest ones." James Lowry, the CEO of AR Battle Systems, an augmented reality company working with the military on large development contracts, stands with drink in hand while his other hand is deep in his pocket, no doubt stroking his insignificant dick in the hopes that he'll become manlier. The Brightman-Cook building houses his company, and he's so slimy that Fran looks at the floor, searching for the wet trail he must have created. She bites back her distaste.

"Hello, James. How nice of you to come. This is Clarke Parson, one of the animators for the game." She does not introduce James properly to Clarke, knowing it will irritate him. He's a typical blowhard, and she doesn't want to draw out this unfortunate conversation. Before she can redirect him, though, Clarke speaks.

"It's a pleasure to meet you, James. I have to get back to work, but I hope you enjoy the game." She turns toward Fran. "I'll catch up with you later?" she asks Fran.

"Of course." Fran nods. She has great plans for seeing her later. Every inch.

"Nice to meet you, Clarke. I hope I'll see you later, too." Although James couches his words in an even, genial tone of voice, they anger Fran. He has some nerve displaying his blatant interest in Clarke. At least Clarke doesn't respond, instead scampering away toward a group of guests, clipboard at the ready.

"She is delectable, isn't she, Fran? Just the type you like."

Anger bubbles beneath her skin as Fran eyes the repugnant man. "Pardon?" She will give him one chance to backpedal. She has dated sporadically over the years, and she certainly does not have a type.

He blanches. "Not that I'd know. I must have confused you with someone else." He perks up, and Fran braces for his next ridiculous statement.

"She's certainly my type, and if she weren't, I'd make an exception. Any chance you'll give me her number?"

She glowers at him. "I'm sure your wife would love that." She turns away, eyes searching for Harry. "If you'll excuse me, I must have a word with my creative director." She walks away without waiting for an answer.

Soon Fran is able to shake off the unfortunate conversation as she's swept up in the excitement, immersed in the game through the guests' eyes. As she walks around the main exhibit, she feels a sense of satisfaction. They worked hard to make this video, particularly once they blended their work with what Runaway Games completed. The product they've released is one of the most realistic available, its graphics and animation more detailed and fluid than any other game they've developed. It's movie-quality, and Fran is well-aware that is due to Clarke's expertise. She constantly amazes her. The night has sped by, and Fran feels on top of the world. Early projections show their sales will smash all competitors' games during the holiday season. She can't wait to celebrate with Clarke.

Hearing a commotion behind her, Fran turns and feels anger suffuse her. She marches over to where Harry is arguing with a tall, willowy woman in a flowing sundress. It doesn't seem to faze her that it's twenty degrees outside. Sig Sassy stands as if she owns the world, an apathetic expression on her face as she gazes around the venue. Fran catches Harry's final words as she joins them on the side of the room.

"You are not welcome here. You need to leave." Harry crosses his arms, glowering at the woman.

"This is a public event, Harry. Let's not blow this out of proportion. I have a ticket to be here, and I want to see the finished version of the hottest game of the year." Sassy tosses her hair back with a jerk of her head, like a filly annoyed by a fly trying to land on her face.

Fran turns to Harry, outraged. "How did she get a ticket?"

Before he can answer, Sig Sassy says, "I bought it online. It's not like I had a choice, thanks to you. I have to say, I'm surprised you're so threatened by my presence. After all, if it weren't for me, you wouldn't even be a part of this release. Instead, the best game of the year would belong to Runaway Games exclusively. So, as a thank you, why don't you let me through?"

Barely able to keep herself from shoving the offensive woman out the door as rage courses through her, Fran says with a firm voice, "No, no. That is not going to happen." She glares at Sassy. "You have some nerve coming here." She steps closer, invading Sassy's space and nearly smirks when she takes a step back. "You are extremely fortunate that we did not sue you after what you did, never mind file a complaint with the DA, but our leniency stemmed from Clarke's tender heart and not any cleverness on your part." She sneers at the woman, leaning in as she lowers her voice. "It would take truly little to destroy you in every way. So far, we've limited our response to letting others in the industry know what you did, but we can and will do so much more if you attempt to stay here."

"What more can you do?" Sassy asks, bitterness seeping from each word. "You blacklisted me. I can't even work internationally. Everyone is hands-off, and I have you to thank."

"That's where you're wrong. The only one you have to thank is yourself. I hope it was worth it, stealing all of Clarke's work with some juvenile attempt to hurt her."

"Who says that's not what I wanted? Huh?" She smirks, cocking her head as she rests a hand on her hip. "She had to reveal how it happened, didn't she? You know she's carried a torch for you all this time. Poor Clarke, infatuated with the frigid Queen of Games. Tell me, did you let her down easy or tell her in that distinct way you have that she'll never have a chance at bedding the devil?"

The glee in those greedy eyes, begging to hear how Fran rejected her, embarrassed her, ripped out Clarke's heart and ate it for lunch infuriates Fran. Her feelings must show on her face as Sassy steps backward, all cockiness gone. Fran's voice shakes as she struggles to control her emotions. "You never deserved her." Her lip curls in derision, and Fran balls her fists at her sides. "If you ever attempt to hurt her again, there's nowhere in the world you'll be able to hide from me. Now, get out." She watches with satisfaction as Sassy scurries away.

"Wow. Another moment under your wrath and I'm sure she would have peed herself." Harry snickers. "Well done. Wait until I tell Clarke."

"You will do no such thing." Taking a deep breath, Fran softens her voice. "At least, not tonight. She has enough on her plate." She glances at her watch. "In fact, it's time for the final rounds of the competition. Shall we go watch?"

Harry stares at her long enough that she feels like a mouse being sized up by a hungry cat. She raises an eyebrow, and he rearranges his expression into jovial conviviality. "Of course. Let's see who wins the game."

As they walk toward the crowded area where watchers are cheering for the players, Fran can't help but believe she is the winner since she has Clarke on her team. Once they arrive, she watches as Clarke yells out tips to the players. She helps the players level up while some of their guests jot down notes, no doubt to try out when they next play the game. One of the finalists makes a poor decision, and hundreds of fish and birds wash up on the oil-slicked Pacific shores as a collective groan permeates the room. Clarke's quick to help the player get back on track.

The event is live-streaming, and when she glances over at the screen, she sees several hundred viewers and a steady flow of comments. This event is an unmitigated success. She feels the sweep of euphoria lifting her higher, as does the idea of removing each item of Clarke's clothing and tasting every delectable inch. Clarke glances at her, her eyes widening and an attractive flush climbing up her throat to tinge her face a lovely shade of red.

Fran has no doubt she transmitted her wayward thoughts to Clarke. No matter. It's good that she understands exactly what Fran has in mind for her tonight. Oh, she might not know the precise details, but she knows they will be together. She knows they will end up wrapped around one another, melding into one entity as they rejoice in their success. In addition, Fran will rejoice in spending more time with Clarke. Sig made the biggest mistake of her life, letting Clarke go. Fran has learned from her own stupidity as well as Sig's, though, and she has no plans on ever letting Clarke walk away from her again.

Chapter Eight

MISCOMMUNICATION

LOOKING AROUND THE RECEPTION area, Clarke smiles faintly as she recognizes some of the best professionals in the videogame industry milling about the room. She feels nerves shoot through her, a giddiness she attributes to working on several projects headed by some of the best minds in the industry. Last year she would not have imagined rubbing elbows with them, yet tonight she receives welcoming smiles and nods of acknowledgement from some of the elite. The Games Awards is always a well-attended event. It's a great way to kick off the new year, and an even better reason to get out of the house during the winter months. Although Clarke is a nominee for Best Narrative, she's under no illusions. She's up against much more complex, multi-platform videogame narrations. Still, it's an honor to be here.

She tries not to shift from foot to foot as she stands with a group of Runaway Games employees. At least her Oxford shoes are comfortable. The shoes are oxblood color and match her silk blouse. She's wearing her favorite black slacks and lucky argyle socks, with a dark tweed jacket completing the look of chic geek. She's noticed that people have dressed in a wide array of styles, some wearing jeans while others wear dresses and suits. She even saw some attendees wearing college sweatshirts. Clarke's glad to note the people in her group have chosen to dress business casual like she has. She has worked with everyone in the group at some point and even gone out for drinks with a few of them. Although she finds small talk tiresome and inside jokes ostracizing, she's able to follow the conversation well enough to nod and chuckle when appropriate. At least she's comfortable enough to not guzzle her glass of Prosecco as if she's a college sorority pledge, so that's something.

Next to her, Sean Bell says, "Look at all these people, Clarke. We're swimming with the big fish now." He looks like a carefree surfer dude or some throwback to the drug-fueled 70s. Nothing could be further from the truth. He's a left-brain guy who likes nothing better than to write code to relax. He's one of the people wearing jeans, although they're in good condition. He's paired the black pants with a maroon sweater over a black turtleneck. When he noticed how they match, he chastised the rest of the group for not getting the notice on what to wear.

Shaking her head with amusement, Clarke looks around the room with interest. Not wanting to attend the event alone and knowing Fran would never deign to accompany her, Clarke latched onto Sean once he mentioned he was attending. He's a nice enough guy, if a bit shallow. Still, Clarke knows he's happily married with two kids. She's also aware that his wife has no interest in video games and wasn't planning on attending tonight's ceremony. Staying close to him provides her with a great buffer, and she knows she can relax while gawking at the attendees. At least she isn't asking for their autographs.

Clarke has worked with Sean on several projects at Runaway Games over the years. He's a game programmer, comfortable being a workhorse at a small company. She's urged him to apply to bigger companies, but he's told her several times that he doesn't want the stress. He likes his life and doesn't want to hate what he does for a living. Joining the industry right after college fifteen years ago, Sean is well-respected and knows everyone. His collar-length blond locks give him a relaxed, boho look, particularly when he wears a man-bun, and his self-effacing grin make him look like he's perpetually high—on drugs or life is anyone's guess. He leads Clarke around, introducing her to various acquaintances from the tech side of the industry, and she feels her nervousness melt away.

Finding herself nursing a drink while she and Sean stand off to the side of the tables, she gasps.

"Everything okay?" Sean asks.

Blinking, Clarke sighs with relief. "Yeah. I thought I saw that asshole, James Lowry. He practically propositioned me at the launch. He's a real winner."

"Ah. It's a good idea to stay away from that one. He has some serious pull in the industry thanks to his connections. You know he works with the military, right?"

Clarke swings her head around to stare at Sean. "Are you serious?"

"Oh, yeah. Word is, he strongarmed certain people to get the contract, if you know what I mean. Of course, the military doesn't care as long as they get what they want, and they want realistic, cutting-edge AR to train incoming recruits, not to mention the reintegration of post-traumatic stress disorder candidates. His company has reaped the benefits, and if he had to remove some people from the game—no, really, Clarke, I'm not exaggerating. His competition disappeared like last week's leftovers."

Clarke releases an incredulous gasp. "I think it's more likely that those leftovers were thrown out by your wife."

"As likely as his competition not having any choice about dropping out of consideration for a contract with the military. And let me tell you, some of those companies were much further along with their augmented reality projects. It doesn't help that he has the ear of those on the Brightman-Cook board of directors. He's gained clout due to the military deal, which means that his company and Haboob end up competing for money to develop their deals." He peers at Clarke. "Be careful with him. Try to stay under the radar. He has a huge ego and likes to have it stroked. It's hard to believe his wife hasn't left him. Maybe it's the money."

They move on to better topics, joining small groups to continue networking. When Clarke ends up discussing animation software with someone who works at DreamWorks, she reminded herself not to squee. She thinks she manages pretty well, at least until she sees the laughter in Sean's eyes. Nevertheless, it's an enjoyable conversation, and they exchange contact information before parting. Too soon the buffet opens, and they join the line to grab some food before finding their seats. She's surprised to find she's famished. Talking to so many people must have helped her work up an appetite. Gobbling down her roast beef, garlic mashed potatoes, and salad as if she hasn't eaten tasty food in years, Clarke clears her plate in record time. She sits back, barely stopping herself from patting her tummy. At least she has the restraint to refuse dessert when servers come around with them.

After the meal, the speeches and presentations begin. Glancing around the room, Clarke cannot help feeling hyper-aware. Shifting her gaze toward the front, Clarke finds herself riveted by a pair of ice-blue eyes. Pointedly, those beloved eyes slide to Clarke's left before returning to her rapidly widening eyes. The raised eyebrows eloquently ask Clarke who the hell is with her. Hearing her name mentioned, Clarke looks around bewildered, glancing at the stage and then at her tablemates as everyone begins to clap.

Sean jumps up and pulls on Clarke's hand to help her rise. "You won!" he exclaims and hugs her enthusiastically. She finds it hard to believe she's won an award. Her category nominated some of the most respected narrators in the industry. This is surreal. Clarke feels a gentle push toward the stage and finally figures out what is happening. She must stow her incredulity into a box for the next few minutes, if only so she doesn't make a fool of herself.

She weaves through the tables to get to the front of the room, careful not to trip over any feet. Once at the podium, Clarke can only focus on how Fran is sitting in front of her with an inscrutable look on her face. She looks like a Roman bust, so still is her expression. Until she looks into eyes that roil with emotion. She feels like prey caught in a snake's powerful gaze. Clarke takes a settling breath and thanks the appropriate people, falling back on speaking from the heart. "Boy, who knew writing poems and fanfiction could lead to this moment? I get to exercise my imagination every day and play with incredible characters, both through creating the graphics and telling their stories. Thank you so much." She hustles off the stage to scattered applause, nodding at anyone who makes eye contact with her.

Sitting at her table a few minutes later, Clarke feels her heartrate slowing down. That was the scariest moment she's ever experienced. Well maybe the second scariest. She won't ever forget her abject fear when she realized she had to send Fran the email about Sig's fraudulent actions. Since no one is looking at her funny, Clarke guesses she didn't say anything absurd when she was on stage. Her hands twitch on her lap, her desire to corner Fran and find out why she seems upset with her making it hard to relax. All she wants to do is talk to Fran, but Clarke knows she will need to wait until the ceremony is over.

Ten thousand years later, Clarke moves her petrified body in slow motion to unbend it. "I'm going to the restroom," Clarke says to Sean before rising from her seat. Not waiting for a reply, Clarke's eyes seek out and find Fran, who is watching her closely. Clarke walks through the hall to reach the door which exits to a wide atrium and waits by the side. A few moments later the door opens, and Fran passes through the doorway, not even looking at Clarke. She's gorgeous in a plum dress that falls above the knees. Her black hosiery highlights toned calves, and Clarke wonders when Fran finds the time to exercise. Without slowing, Fran strides through the hall that circles a large staircase and enters an empty conference room on the side with Clarke in pursuit.

As soon as Clarke closes the door, Fran rounds on her, hissing her words. "Is there something I should know, Clarke?"

Startled by the anger threaded through the question, Clarke stares at Fran. She doesn't know how to answer. *Why is she upset? What did I do?*

"I see." Fran's eyes harden into diamond chips as her stance straightens. She pulls on the hem of each long sleeve before swiping down her thighs, her anger prevalent in each motion as she seems to wipe away their connection while straightening up.

It's obvious Fran misconstrues her hesitation, and Clarke fears she will march out of the room without saying another word. She raises her hands in defense as a memory of Fran's eyes sliding to Sean flashes through her mind. The idea that Fran is jealous is absurd, and as Fran takes a step toward the door, she nearly shouts, "No. He's just a friend, a colleague from work. I didn't want to come here alone." Clarke doesn't know what to do, what to say to convince Fran. If she loses her—

Fran's sneering voice catches Clarke's attention. "And the fact that he's been showing you off, introducing you to everyone like you're some coveted prize. Did it never occur to you how that would be interpreted?" The overhead lights reflect off blazing eyes intent on slicing through Clarke.

"Fran!" Clarke exclaims, her hand covering her heart. "I didn't even know you'd be here—"

"Yes, I suppose it would have been much more convenient if I had not witnessed such a spectacle." Fran's eyes are wild, her body trembling and hands squeezed into tight fists. She's barely holding herself together, and Clarke is unsure how to de-escalate the situation. She hasn't done anything wrong.

"There was nothing to witness." Clarke realizes she's raised her voice again and takes a deep breath. In a softer voice, she says, "I would never cheat on you. Don't you know me at all?" Clarke wrings her hands.

"Obviously not if you go flouncing about town with pretty boys like some slut when we're not together." As Fran spits out the poisonous words, her eyes narrow into slits.

"I do not, I am not," Clarke sputters. She's becoming rather upset at this unjustified display. It's not like Fran has ever indicated she's willing to go public. If anything, Clarke is Fran's dirty secret. Although Fran is the one who told the powerful industry players that Clarke is worth hiring, she understands why Fran won't attend industry events with her. It would reveal a connection not usual for a CEO and a worker bee.

"I suppose it never occurred to you to invite me." Not a question.

"Oh, come on, Fran. Why would I set myself up for rejection like that? You compartmentalize me in your life like you do to your work, your friends, your personal life. I provide this secret service for you, and you have me so twisted around your little finger that I'm willing to take whatever time you condescend to grant me. I lick the soles of your expensive shoes every chance I get, and I'm grateful for the chance. I'm pathetic." Seeing Fran's pale face and trembling frame, Clarke moves away from her. She is unable to stand being so close to her while she shakes with rage. Clarke knows that if she wants any chance of salvaging this misunderstanding, she needs to stop feeling sorry for herself and remember how fortunate she is to have Fran spend any time with her. It's better to know her place in Fran's world and not delude herself.

"We both know you never would have come here with me, Fran," Clarke adds quietly. It costs her greatly to voice this truth. It tears at her because she knows she'll never be good enough to be on Fran's arm. Meeting at restaurants can be easily explained, working on video games for Haboob doesn't raise eyebrows, but attending high-profile events together is entirely different. Although Clarke has accomplished much in six years, she's not foolish enough to believe they are equals.

"Well. We'll never know, will we?"

Clarke's head shoots up and she stares at Fran, uncertain what she means. Fran sounds hurt. *Is she breaking up with me?* That can't happen. Clarke doesn't know how she can go back to a life without her.

"I—Fran. If you only knew how much I wanted you next to me tonight, how much I will always want to be by your side…I'm sorry I didn't at least ask." Clarke's voice cracks as Fran waves dismissively and turns away. Clarke feels ice slide down her spine. She's scared. Somehow, she needs to make Fran understand.

Approaching her slowly, Clarke takes a chance and pulls her into a fierce hug. She feels Fran's body meld into hers as arms wind around her waist. Relieved beyond belief, Clarke takes deep breaths to calm down.

"I really am sorry," Clarke murmurs. She feels like shit. "I didn't realize it was a possibility."

"I know. I understand why this happened." Fran sighs and pulls Clarke more closely to her. "I do care about you, Clarke," Fran murmurs. She brushes her nose across the shell of Clarke's ear and kisses it when Clarke shudders. Fran nibbles on the lobe, much to Clarke's delight. She takes solace in Fran's attention. "Congratulations on your win. I didn't realize you write poems."

"Thanks." Clarke moans at the feeling of wet lips sliding down her neck and stalling on her pulse point. "Writing poems helps me relax." She doesn't add that they help her process her feelings for Fran. "Congratulations on your wins. Haboob racked them up."

"Hopefully next year we'll win Game of the Year with *End of the World*. It's what brought us together." Fran pulls back to gaze at Clarke. "Perhaps you'll allow me to read your poetry some time."

A frisson of fear sweeps through Clarke at the thought of Fran reading her innermost thoughts. She swallows down her apprehension and nods. They stand together, allowing their spat to fade away. Clarke's mind blanks as she takes comfort in the moment. She nearly jumps when Fran breaks the silence.

"I saw you that day you sent me the email on Sassy." Fran's whisper fills the room. "You were on the sidewalk speaking to Harry, and I knew. I knew I wanted to see you again." Clarke feels silky lips slide across her collarbones. "Then you sent me that email, and I saw my opportunity."

Clarke pulls away to see Fran's face. She seems vulnerable. "I'm glad you did. I am. I've never been able to get over you. Six years apart and not a day has passed without you in my thoughts, no matter how I've tried to forget you." Clarke wonders whether she should be revealing herself so much, but she's still reeling from the possibility of losing this, losing Fran.

Fran stares at Clarke as if trying to impart some momentous truth, some startling secret of the world, some—

"Come home with me, Clarke?"

Oh. Well, that's pretty damn wonderful, too. "Yes." Clarke will figure out some excuse to offer her colleagues. She's glad she'll be in Fran's arms again tonight.

And it's as simple as that.

Chapter Nine

THE ROMANCE

OVER THE NEXT FEW months, they fall into a rhythm where Fran invites Clarke to a meal, and they return to her chic apartment to make love afterward. Whenever the meal is breakfast or lunch, Fran always returns to work later in the day. When the shared meal is dinner, Clarke wakes up the next morning alone. Nevertheless, Clarke loves dinners the best since they have more time together, and she gets to fall asleep in Fran's arms. She dreams of waking up this way, too. Clarke is hopeful that one day her dreams will become reality. She knows she must be patient and not make demands.

Slowly, slight changes occur. Fran begins to confide in Clarke about matters closer to her heart. She talks about her fears for her daughter's future, the direction of the company, her desire to renovate the apartment, and her plans to take a vacation. The last subject surprises Clarke. She can't remember ever hearing about Fran taking vacations. Not even with her daughter. Perhaps that began after Clarke left Haboob Software.

"Is there any destination you wish to visit but have not yet?" Fran asks as she sips her wine. They are having dinner at an exclusive Italian restaurant in Soho. They are ensconced in a cozy booth toward the back of the restaurant where the lighting is dim enough to create an intimate ambiance. It casts interesting shadows across the table, making everything seem mysterious and appealing. More enticing to Clarke is how the scant illumination emphasizes Fran's cheeks and chin while obscuring the blue of her eyes.

"Me?" Clarke feels like a mouse squeaking out the word to the cat as she swishes her tail. She reacts this way too often to Fran's questions, but Fran seems amused rather than annoyed. Clarke wipes off the spattered alfredo sauce from her sleeve, scowling at how clumsy she gets when nervous. It figures. She just bought the new blouse to impress Fran, not that she seems to care. Maybe it's due to the low lighting, which is unfortunate since its gold color complements Clarke's eyes and hair. In the grand scheme of things, it doesn't matter. No matter how she dresses, it doesn't cancel out the butterflies in her stomach.

She thought she'd stop feeling this way after spending more time with Fran, but instead of becoming suave and sophisticated, she remains a bumbling fool around her. She takes a quick sip of her wine to clear her throat and buy herself a bit more time. "Um, well, there are tons of places I'd like to visit. Italy, England, Scotland, Switzerland, any of the Caribbean islands—I haven't really been anywhere except San Francisco when you took all the interns to the annual game summit. As you know, I'm going to Albany next week for some classes, but I won't have any time to explore. Hell, I'd be happy going to Miami or San Diego." All true. It's one of the negatives of working as a freelancer—she has no way to recoup her expenses for industry conferences and continuing education. She doesn't have the funds to travel for pleasure, as she must save her money for work-related trips or short visits to her parents. She doesn't even own a car—not that she needs one in The City. Before she came to New York, she always borrowed her parents' car when she needed to drive somewhere.

Fran chuckles. "I'm sure you'll have the opportunity to visit many of those places, Clarke." The way she says it sounds so certain that Clarke has no choice but to believe her.

"I hope so. Now that I'm starting to make more money, I can save for them." She notices a strange look cross Fran's face, but before she can ask what she's thinking, her face clears, and she hums her agreement. Clarke decides it mustn't be important. Otherwise, Fran would say something. It's not like she ever edits herself. *Maybe she thinks I won't earn enough money as soon as I think.*

"How about you? Is there anywhere you haven't visited yet?"

"As I'm sure you can guess, I've been to many places around the globe, but most of those trips were work-related. I believe revisiting some of those destinations for recreation would create entirely new experiences for me. Nor am I opposed to visiting some place new. I hear the sunsets are spectacular on some of the Caribbean islands."

"That sounds terrific. I've always wanted to vacation on one of those islands. Sunbathe, swim in those beautiful waters, maybe a sunset cruise. Sometimes the daily grind can really wear me down. Not that I'm complaining about all the work I have. You must know how grateful I am to you."

"Don't be ridiculous. You've earned all those projects. I did nothing other than let others know of your integrity and sense of fairness. It is no surprise that others are quick to offer you projects because you are hard-working and trustworthy."

Flabbergasted, Clarke stares with wide eyes at Fran. She shakes her head, thoughts racing. Fran isn't known to throw around compliments—people must earn them. "Thank you, Fran. That means so much coming from you." Throat parched, Clarke swallows most of the water in her goblet, resisting the urge to place the sweating crystal against her forehead. When she glances at Fran, she's captivated by the tender look in her blue eyes.

Once they return to Fran's home, they shelve all discussions about vacations in favor of more elemental communication. They've made love enough times that she can read Fran's body and anticipate what she needs. It amazes her when she sees the proof of Fran's passion for her, the woman who is known in the industry as a person who has little patience for incompetence. She takes what she wants without apology, and although Clarke wasn't surprised to find this has bled over into the bedroom, she doesn't mind in the least. Fran's ardor rouses Clarke's hunger, and the only way to feel satiated is to slake Fran's thirst. It makes her think of a poem she wrote after their previous encounter, a week ago, which she titled "Yours."

Brushing past softly
Circling back for more
Opening up to you—I focus
Drinking you in more and more.
Sparring, wrestling, submitting,
Lips, eyes, soul: I am yours.

Clarke's eyes flutter closed, the combination of tonight's lovemaking and memories of the last time combining into a heady blanket of satisfaction. She falls further in love with Fran each time they're together. It's getting harder to resist declaring it to Fran and the rest of the world, ramifications be damned. Those thoughts are insane, though. She will not jeopardize their tenuous relationship by revealing the extent of her feelings before Fran indicates in some way that she feels the same.

Although Fran is noticeably absent when Clarke awakens the next morning, she finds a flower on the pillow next to her. Fran started this sweet gesture a few weeks ago. The first time, she found a red rose, and it lit her up like the sun breaking through the clouds. She was so ebullient that a colleague nicknamed her Sunshine. The next time she spent the night, she found a sunflower. Last week she woke up to a vibrant pink camellia. Not that she recognized what type of flower it was. She had to look it up.

Fran also leaves clothes for her, like the softest flannel shirt she's ever felt and graphic T-shirts of bands she enjoys. It's become quite clear how closely Fran pays attention to everything Clarke says, even her passing comments about songs she loves. Three days ago, Fran left black lingerie that made her breathless. These actions let Clarke know their relationship is not casual, just gradual.

Sometimes Clarke wakes up in the middle of the night to find Fran watching her. At such times Clarke pulls her in for a long hug before turning her gently so she can spoon her. Although they never speak during such moments, Clarke finds she doesn't mind. She knows when Fran is ready, she'll open up. In the meantime, Clarke does her best to show how much she loves the time they spend together.

At lunch a few days later, Fran surprises Clarke by saying, "Elaine will be home for spring break in two weeks. She wants to meet you." Her expression is carefully neutral as she waits for Clarke to respond.

Clarke jumps at the chance. "That sounds great. I'd love to meet her." Nervous energy races through her. Even though Elaine's campus is relatively close, Clarke has not met her since she worked at Haboob Software. If Elaine wants to meet her, that must mean Fran has talked about her. She wonders what she's told her daughter. *How should I act? What if Elaine doesn't like me?* Clarke startles when she feels a hand covering hers. Looking up, she gazes into reassuring eyes. They settle her.

"Have faith, Clarke. She remembers you from the few times you interacted when she was a child. She's grown into a mature, thoughtful young woman. You have nothing to fear." Clarke feels Fran's hand squeeze hers before releasing it.

After Clarke's resolute nod, Fran suggests dinner at the apartment on the Saturday that Elaine will be home. Clarke takes out her cell phone and marks her calendar, so she won't forget.

They finish their meal while talking about Elaine, Clarke's curiosity urging her to ask questions. She wants to have some idea of who she's become and what interests her. Fran is generous with her information, taking the time to explain about Elaine's upbringing, hobbies, college classes, and personality traits. Fran's adoration for her daughter is obvious, as she regales Clarke with several stories about her childhood.

Clarke believes they have become closer over the months, that Fran has lowered her defenses. More often now they discuss their lives, their families. Clarke has yet to tell Fran about her falling out with her family, though. She doesn't want to explain why. She doesn't want to discuss how afraid she is that they will have another fight once her parents find out she's seeing Fran. She knows if she must choose, she will choose Fran, and that scares her, too. She fears Fran will tire of her eventually and send her away. She has many fears, and sometimes it's all she can do to stuff them down and act as if she's content with hiding so much of herself from those she loves. She's quick to remind herself that it's worth it. She's grateful for all the time she's spent with Fran. She will take every moment she's given with her and guard each memory jealously.

When they make love after lunch, it's intense. They keep their eyes trained on one another, breasts rubbing and centers gyrating together, hands linked on either side of Fran's head. As they reach toward their orgasms, they struggle to retain their visual connection. Clarke sobs Fran's name as she climaxes, feeling herself pulled into a gentle embrace. She hears her name repeated over and over, and all she can do is cling to her. Clarke loves this woman so much. She has to believe Fran cares for her, certainly enough to allow her daughter to spend time with her. She relaxes as she feels Fran's hands drawing circles on her back. Yes, she cares. She must.

***

Dinner isn't as scary as Clarke imagined. Elaine is a bright twenty-something studying business management. Although introspective and quiet, she becomes quite spirited when she's relaxed. She fills the dinner conversation with stories of her experiences on campus, in her classes, and meeting new friends.

Clarke feels a bit nostalgic, remembering a simpler time when all she had to do was be open to the possibilities that life presented to her. She's fascinated while watching Fran interact with her daughter. It's obvious how much she has missed her. She doubts anyone at Haboob has seen her this mellow and happy. Except Harry. Maybe.

Clarke knows that Elaine is studious and hard-working college student. She's already lined up a summer internship on Wall Street, and she's full of ideas for future businesses. She wants to create more jobs in the tech industry for females, an idea Clarke can get behind wholeheartedly. She knows Fran will do everything she can to help her daughter, provided Elaine accepts the help. She has a good head on her shoulders, and unlike so many idealistic young women, she understands that sometimes an introduction to the right person can open closed doors for her. That's a lesson Clarke learned early in her career, and Fran's actions reinforced it after she warned Fran about Sig.

By the end of the evening, Clarke is confident Elaine likes her. As the night progressed, Elaine asked about her interests. Clarke barely refrained from mentioning Fran as number one on her list, her favorite foods, and entertainment. Clarke's relieved to find that they share many of the same tastes. Even better, Fran's tastes align with hers. The more common ground they have, the better chance Clarke has to remain a part of the Silvetti household. Her favorite part of the evening by far is when Elaine tells her stories about her teen years with Fran. By then, Fran's husband had died of a heart attack, and they'd forged a close bond while grieving their loss.

"And when Mom came in and saw the mess, I thought she was going to kill me," Elaine says, hands held before her in the classic 'wait-for-it' pantomime. "I'm sure you've discovered by now that Mom is nothing if not unpredictable. Instead of ripping me a new one, she nearly fell on the floor, she was laughing so hard. When she saw my face—and believe me when I say I was shocked stupid—she pulled out her phone and took a picture. Can you believe it?"

Laughing not only at the story but also at the way Elaine tells it, Clarke shakes her head. "I can only imagine."

"How could I be upset? It's not as if she meant to get tomato sauce on the ceilings. And walls. And floors." Fran chuckles. "I count it among one of the best Mother's Days I've ever experienced." She glances at Clarke and a cheeky grin alerts her that she's about to tease her daughter. "Elaine didn't realize how much cleaning she'd end up doing that day in addition to the homemade meal."

"Yeah. Homemade ravioli and sauce turned into peanut butter sandwiches."

"And they were delicious."

Clarke watches them smile and feels her own lips curl up. She loves watching Fran interact with Elaine. Her comportment changes completely; it's as if she's another person. Her body is loose, forearms resting on the table, and eyes bright. She looks nothing like the complicated, formidable business mogul she's known to be outside of her home. The insight Clarke's gained through the stories Elaine has shared tonight are priceless.

When they decide to call it a night, Elaine pulls Clarke aside. "It was great to finally meet you properly. I vaguely remember meeting you when I was around fourteen, but that time in my life is a bit hazy. Whenever I think back to those years after Dad died, it's like I'm watching a movie. "

"I can't imagine what that felt like. I do remember you came by Haboob one time, though, and you were so polite and quiet. Nothing like tonight." She grins when Elaine's mouth drops open. "Just kidding."

"Ha-ha. I'm sure it's not your sense of humor that Mom likes." It's her turn to grin at Clarke's reaction. "Seriously, I think you're good for her, Clarke. She seems calmer. Happier." Her grin widens into a smile, and Clarke smiles back warmly.

"I'm glad. I like spending time with her, and I've enjoyed getting to know you." Elaine hugs her before hustling to her room.

Clarke isn't looking by then. She has locked eyes with Fran, who remains still, head cocked, as her eyes roam Clarke's body. She shivers with anticipation. She swears Fran was a cougar in a past life, what with the way she stalks toward Clarke with such focused intent. Clarke is faint with desire by the time Fran reaches her. Clarke's sweater feels heavy, her body hot enough that she has to restrain herself from pulling the collar away from her neck. Her breathing speeds up when Fran takes her hand to lead her upstairs.

Although it astounds Clarke, their lovemaking is even better, even more poignant. They have turned a corner. Clarke perceives that Fran's daughter has accepted her, and this has cemented her relationship with Fran in some way. Fran worships Clarke's body as she did the first time they made love—undressing her slowly, kissing every part of her, taking the time to make Clarke feel cherished. And after Clarke comes down from the stratosphere, Fran makes love to her again, holding her close afterward while running her fingers through Clarke's hair the way she loves until she falls into an exhausted sleep.

Chapter Ten

THE NEXT STEP

SIGHING, FRAN OPENS HER eyes to the winter morning. Heat radiates down her left side, and a smile lights up her face as she turns to gaze at the sleeping figure. Clarke. Sweet Clarke. She looks so innocent, so young. It has not escaped her notice that Clarke is much closer in age to her daughter than to her. It used to bother her, lusting after a younger woman.

It's not that she's a vain woman. She eats right and exercises. Still, she's fifteen years older than Clarke. It takes her longer to rebound from a strenuous workout or vigorous lovemaking. She isn't as flexible as she was at Clarke's age. Even ignoring the physical differences which occur with age, Fran had worried that they were too far apart in their careers, their life perspectives, and their experiences to make a successful go at a relationship. At least, that's what she told herself when she sent Clarke off with a recommendation and good wishes so long ago. That's what she told herself every time Clarke's name popped up at work, or her smiling face swam across her mind, or peers bandied Clarke's name around on the award circuit. None of that mattered once Clarke contacted her. When she received the email about Sassy, she realized she didn't care about the age gap. She didn't care about the disparity in their job positions. She didn't care that she was born in the 70's and Clarke was born in the 90's. She didn't care about anything other than the feelings Clarke stirred in her. Still stirs in her. She decided to take the chance, and it's the best decision she's ever made.

Last night they enjoyed dinner together for the first time with Elaine. At the end of the meal, her daughter made sure to tell her how much she likes Clarke. Her acceptance means the world to Fran. Although she knew in her heart that her daughter would love Clarke, she cannot deny how anxious she felt. Clarke means so much to her. Caressing the woman's face with her eyes, she feels warmth flow through her. She loves Clarke. The last four months have confirmed what she always suspected. She cannot go back to living without Clarke in her life. She shivers as fear slices through her, and she barely resists pulling Clarke into her arms to warm herself.

Before this *thing* began, she followed Clarke's career progression and listened to the softly spoken words around the office, straining to hear scraps of information about Clarke. She fed on those scraps like a starving dog, missing her but too insecure and proud to reach out, to take the chance. Such a waste of time. Years they could have lived happily together.

It was a shock when she noticed the telltale signs that Clarke returned her interest. Fran thought she was doing what was best for everyone by not hiring her after the internship ended. Not with those eyes revealing her attraction. Not with her at the beginning of her career. Not with so many opportunities waiting for Clarke's notice. The woman was a temptation, and Fran wasn't ready to open herself up to anyone, not even to the possibility of happiness. She told herself she needed to focus on Elaine, on Haboob, on the latest projects. They were all excuses, ridiculous rationalizations. The truth was that she let Clarke go because she knew, at some instinctual level, that she would never be the same once she tasted her lips, touched her skin. And she was right.

When her husband, Derek, died a couple of years before Clarke entered her world, Fran created a routine that consisted of work and time with her daughter. The way Clarke intrigued her after becoming her intern was shocking. Her libido ramped up, and Fran found herself thinking about the wet-behind-the-ears intern with the sharp mind and flexible imagination. Nowadays, she's one of the most gifted graphic designers in the business, and with her animation skills, she could easily take on responsibilities at more prestigious development companies. With some nudging by Fran, she's glad to see that others are taking notice.

The fear she harbored all those years ago is no longer present. She's tired of letting it rule her actions. She grimaces when she remembers her poor reaction to seeing Clarke at the awards ceremony with a colleague. Her behavior was abhorrent, as were some of the words she spewed. Clarke was magnanimous enough to ignore her insults, much to Fran's relief. Well, perhaps not. It's more likely she believed she was at fault, but Fran knows the truth. As much as she believes Clarke cares for her, may even love her, she has not said as much. Nor has she done much to reveal her feelings, other than to accept Fran's advances. When Fran thinks about Clarke's unwillingness to take an active role in defining their relationship, she becomes insecure. Not once has Clarke invited her out or initiated intimacy. That must change.

It's time. Time for Clarke to stand beside her. Time for her to step up in their relationship. Fran knows Clarke is afraid, knows she's taking whatever Fran gives her without demands or complaints, but their relationship cannot grow while Clarke hangs back. She needs Clarke, wants Clarke, as more than a lover.

And she knows actions speak louder than words. It is why she was so forward with Clarke when they met for dinner months ago. It's why she takes the time to send flowers and invitations. It's why she is never beside Clarke when she wakes in the morning. Not until Clarke has committed to her will she remain. It would break her heart if, after allowing herself to be so vulnerable, Clarke changed her mind. It was hard enough to let her go after her internship ended. That was an altruistic choice Fran made to give Clarke the chance to fly free. Fran isn't strong enough to let her leave again.

The morning light is harsh and unforgiving. She has dreaded the day when Clarke might see her, face free of makeup with her wrinkles revealed—bared to such a young, beautiful creature. She cannot take the chance of seeing anything other than affection and acceptance in those chocolate eyes. So, she waits, searching for a sign that Clarke is ready, that they are ready.

Fran is sure Clarke has drawn her own conclusions as to why she always rises before she awakens. She has read the confusion and uncertainty in her eyes. Yet Clarke has never asked, never demanded an explanation, perhaps afraid of the answer.

Today Fran is ready to at least make a token gesture to signify things will change. Although she will not remain lounging in bed, waiting for Clarke to open her beautiful eyes, she will also not leave Clarke to her own devices this morning. Her daughter has accepted her feelings for Clarke, and Fran can think of nothing preventing her from risking her heart other than fear. And wasn't it her fear which kept them apart for so long?

Carefully, Fran rises from the bed, dons some nightwear, and wraps her robe around her body before leaving the room. She makes her way to the kitchen, pausing in the doorway when she smells fresh coffee. "Elaine?" Fran watches her daughter as she raises her head from its resting place on crossed arms. She looks like she dozed off at the kitchen table. "What are you doing up so early?"

"Couldn't sleep." Elaine yawns. Fran watches her grab the steaming cup of coffee in front of her and drink a large gulp before asking, "Why are you up?"

"I always wake up at this time." Fran sighs as she fills her own cup.

"Yeah, but why aren't you still in bed? Clarke's here, right?" Elaine smirks and wiggles her eyebrows.

"None of that," Fran says with a severe voice. She will not allow such cheek, not even from her beloved daughter.

"Sorry, Mom," Elaine says, her eyes skittering away. "I was just teasing. I can tell she makes you happy, and that's all I want for you."

Sighing, Fran sits across from her daughter. "No, I'm sorry. She's still asleep," Fran says, her voice quiet. "I'm going to make breakfast for her. Do you want anything?"

"Breakfast in bed?" Elaine says, her eyes shining mischievously. "Lucky lady." Her face takes on a more serious expression. "And so are you. It's obvious she loves you."

Touching the back of her hair and glancing at the clock on the microwave, Fran nods. "I, yes. Well. I've told you how I feel about her. Why I have taken this chance." Feeling herself become emotional, she rises quickly and crosses to the refrigerator. "Breakfast," she says in a soft voice, making herself focus on cooking as her embarrassment slowly fades.

Her daughter is an adult now, able to understand romantic entanglements and the inherent complexities that come with trusting someone to such an extent. Her approval is important to Fran. Even though she is a college student, once the press finds out about Clarke, their relationship will become fodder, and that will affect all their lives. As one of the few female CEOs in a predominantly male industry, her personal life is prime real estate for the ravenous horde of reporters hoping to provoke them into saying something they might regret. They will be frothing at the mouth once word gets out of her new romance. She's surprised to find that she doesn't care what they say about her. As she examines her internal landscape and feels nothing but jubilation for having Clarke in her life, relief flows through her. She feels a bit giddy. She realizes quite suddenly that she's happy. Genuinely happy. And it is all due to the sleeping beauty upstairs.

When she first began seeing Clarke, she knew she needed to tell her daughter. Although the media might not guess the nature of her relationship with Clarke, Elaine would. Over the years, Clarke's name came up many times. Her daughter had taken a shine to Clarke after meeting her at the office, and she noticed when Clarke was no longer sitting in the pit at Haboob. She also noticed how lost Fran was. Although young, Elaine recognized something was hurting her.

As time passed and Fran continued to struggle, Elaine asked about her work, the projects and, more tellingly, the people who worked at Haboob. Eventually her inquisitive mind and endless questions uncovered Clarke's desertion. Not that Fran phrased it that way. Not that Clarke truly deserted her. She revealed how Clarke had moved on to become a freelancer with a good recommendation, and she wished her former intern well. Maybe that was what gave her away.

Her no-nonsense attitude and high expectations drove her employees to either produce what she needed or to leave her team. She did not suffer fools or those who wasted her time. Her reputation became legendary as a hard ass, the Queen of Games, a heartless devil. Oh, the monikers were endless and uninspired. Still, she leaned into them since they helped to keep aspiring up-and-comers in line and competitors at bay. She has taken any advantage she can to remain at the top of her industry. If she became a bit more vicious, a bit more short-fused and less flexible after Clarke left her employ, no one figured out why. Except Elaine.

Elaine didn't bring up Clarke's name after that for some months, but she watched Fran and took pains to make her happier. She dedicated herself to practicing the piano without complaint and finishing her schoolwork without help. And every so often, she would mention Clarke, a question about a project Clarke worked on or a memory of an interaction with her while she was Fran's intern. Elaine grew up before Fran's eyes, and they became extremely close. If ever a silver lining existed, it was the compassion and unflagging love her daughter developed. So when Clarke returned, Fran confided in Elaine. She told her what happened and her plans to keep Clarke in her life.

Shaking her head, Fran remembers Elaine's enthusiastic reaction. "It took you long enough. Go get your girl. Let yourself be happy." That little push was all the incentive she needed.

Armed with breakfast, Fran takes a deep breath before making her way upstairs and opening her bedroom door. She enters slowly in case Clarke is still asleep. As she turns back from the door, she sees wide chocolate eyes staring at her, emotions revealing themselves like slides illuminated by a projector. Confusion. Disbelief. Shock. Joy. Placing the tray on the floor, Fran leans over and kisses Clarke. She takes her time, giving her the chance to catch up, to accept this change in their lives. Once she feels Clarke kissing her back with an exuberance that echoes through every inch of Fran's body, she indulges for a few more moments before pulling back.

Loving the dazed happiness Clarke projects as her eyes flutter open, Fran's lips quirk up as she drawls, "Good morning, Clarke." Clarke's adorable, shy demeanor as she answers with her own greeting wraps around Fran's heart. She doesn't try to stop her smile from broadening when Clarke gently pushes back a lock of her white hair which has slipped in front of her eyes. Fran catches her hand and kisses the back of it reverently before turning to pick up the breakfast tray. She places it over Clarke's legs and slips back under the covers. Glancing at Clarke, she's caught by luminous, sparkling eyes. She cannot help but smile again. They proceed to share breakfast quietly, discussing last night's dinner and plans for the day.

"We are planning to see *Wicked* at the Gershwin Theatre today," Fran says as she sips her coffee. "Would you like to join us? We can eat at that tourist trap you love so much afterward." She studies Clarke's reaction, wondering whether she will understand how grand a gesture she is making. Her willingness to share with Clarke this precious time she has with her daughter is no small act. Time with Elaine has become limited as she fills it with school, friends, work, and exploration. She's young and unafraid of the future. And remarkably busy living life.

It occurred to Fran the previous night, as she lay in bed gazing at Clarke's sleeping form, that they have fallen into the bad habit of always meeting for a meal before returning to Fran's home to be intimate. They do not spend time together just for the sake of relaxing or talking or sharing. Fran wants to change that. She wants more than meals and sex. She wants Clarke to impose herself into her life, to make demands and not fit so neatly into her schedule. She wants some overlap, some unexpected interactions, some proof that Clarke is willing to fight for their future. She wants Clarke to call her, and ask her on dates, and invite her into her home. She wants to hear about Clarke's family and friends and poetry.

So, two grand gestures today—surely some type of record for Fran. What Clarke does to her. She inspires Fran to want to take risks. To make these grand gestures for both of them. To push through her fear. And Clarke's fear.

She is beginning to believe Clarke will never make a grand gesture herself, and perhaps that is Fran's fault. She has never given Clarke a reason to ask for more. She has never made Clarke feel safe. She has never reassured her by word or deed. Fran is at a loss. She cannot find the words, and Clarke has not interpreted her actions as enough of a reason to take risks. No matter how slowly and tenderly she makes love to Clarke or how passionately and thoroughly, her actions are not enough. They do not extend outside the bedroom, and consequently, her world is lonely and incomplete.

"I would love to," Clarke says, and hope fills Fran.

It is a start, and although she dearly wants to make love to Clarke right now, she instead tangles their fingers together and asks her about her current project. She needs to take small steps to avoid spooking her. And self-control. Lots of self-control. She will open herself up more, become more transparent, with the hope Clarke will reciprocate. She's playing the long game here, and the stakes are too high for her to make a mistake like pushing Clarke too much or making too many demands. It's a process, building trust, and Fran is willing to be patient. She has the girl. She will not watch her walk away.

Chapter Eleven

ABSENCE MAKES THE HEART GROW FONDER

WHEN CLARKE GETS TO work on Monday, she must fight hard to keep the goofy smile off her face. She feels surer of her relationship with Fran than ever before. Fran was up again before Clarke this morning, but it doesn't bother her quite as much this time since she distinctly remembers soft lips kissing her cheek as she cuddled a Fran-scented pillow.

While speaking to Harry the next day, she tries to sound nonchalant when Fran's name comes up in conversation. She knows it's becoming harder for her to hide her feelings. The love she feels is all-consuming.

"I've noticed a change in Fran's behavior," Harry says.

"Yeah?" Clarke asks in confusion. She hears a big sigh across the phone line.

"The woman seems positively giddy. Not that she's any less of a slavedriver, of course. Between you and me, I think she's dating someone."

"Oh?" Clarke titters. "Um, you think? When would she have the time? Doesn't she work constantly? And didn't you tell me she lost interest in dating years ago?"

"Well, someone's rekindled her fire." His chuckle echoes through the line. "I wish I knew who the new love interest is. Maybe I'll follow her one night and see whether anyone meets her."

"You can't do that! It's such an invasion of privacy. That's crazy. She'd kill you if she saw you." Clarke peters out, knowing how over-the-top she sounds. She feels sweat build at the nape of her neck. The thought of Harry or anyone else discovering their secret is horrifying. Fran might break up with her if anyone finds out. She doesn't think she can go back to a life without her in it.

A long silence on the other line emphasizes her idiocy. "You still have feelings for her." The finality in Harry's voice discourages her from denying the truth, but she tries anyway.

"What? Feelings? Are you nuts? No way. I don't have, I don't know what, I—" A tsking noise interrupts her pathetic attempt to deny her feelings.

"Oh, hon. I thought you'd gotten over that power-crush years ago. I never should have told you she dated a few women after you left Haboob. Maybe being in touch with her reignited your feelings. You know it won't go anywhere, right?" His sympathy seems condescending, and Clarke fights her desire to tell him exactly how far it's gone.

"Of course. She's way out of my league." It hurts her to say the words. She perks up, though, as she thinks about how in touch she truly is with Fran. Oh yes, she loves being in touch with her.

"It's okay. Better people than you have fallen for her charm. You'll get over it. I'll fix you up with someone more your type."

Clarke bites her lip, not wanting to snap at her friend. She knows he means well. "That's sweet of you, but it's probably better that I focus on my projects. I'm glad the launch was successful, so we can get on with our lives."

"Yeah." He chortles. "And you thought she'd eat you up when you sent her that information." Harry's back to teasing her, but Clarke doesn't mind. It means she's no longer in danger of Harry needling her about her feelings.

"Ha-ha. How 'bout that." Clarke's mind immediately goes to how Fran not only eats her up, but makes it feel heavenly. Clarke gulps.

"Speaking of Sig, you do know that Fran destroyed any chance for her to get work in our industry, don't you?"

"Well, I figured she'd let Sig know she was caught…"

"More than that. A few days after you sent the information to Fran, she called a team meeting and invited Sig to the office on the pretext of reviewing some of the storyline. You should have seen her face when she saw everyone staring at her. She looked like the wicked witch watching in horror as a tsunami bore down on her."

"I would've paid to see that." Clarke feels a thrill shoot through her. She remembers witnessing Fran rip people apart for the smallest infractions, always having to do with the work quality. Her words were lethal. She'd experienced one such dressing down early in her internship for failing to create shadowing which corresponded with the story's setting. Clarke created the shadowing as she knew it in New York instead of incorporating the country where the characters were fighting for their lives. She shudders, still remembering Fran's creative flair while asking her whether she ever took an art class in her life, and if so, whether her instructor was blind or smitten. Fran also asked whether Clarke finished high school since she seemed to have no idea about time zones, and climate changes, and the Earth's rotation. It was the last time Clarke failed to research every aspect of a project.

Harry continues with the story, not noticing how Clarke has meandered down memory lane. It's one of the perks of talking on the phone instead of in person. "Sig couldn't remember many of the story points, even though she claimed to pen them. Fran asked more detail-oriented questions that only the author could know—not so much the story's plot but rather the characters' motivations and backgrounds. Well, you know. You've dabbled in writing over the years, and didn't you major in writing for your undergraduate degree?"

"Yup."

"I thought so. I read somewhere that writers only put to paper about ten percent of what they've created for a character's background. If Sig were the writer, she should have been able to answer Fran's questions."

"Yeah. That sounds like one of my nightmares where I'm on stage and don't know what I'm supposed to do for the audience."

"And you're naked, and it's cold, and the audience starts shouting at you?"

Guffawing, Clarke shakes her head. "Um, no. Your anxiety dream sounds much worse."

"Anyway, after it became clear that she was an imposter, Fran really let her have it. I'm talking about comparing her to the lowest of the low, a swindler, oh—Fran was furious. She said, and I quote, 'It's better to let people think you're an Idiot than to open your mouth and prove it.' Her insults only got better. By the time Fran was done with Sig, it was as if she'd sliced her apart with a Ginsu knife."

"Oh my god." Clarke raises a hand to her mouth, eyes widening with shock.

"I haven't seen her so irate in years. She called Sig an oxygen thief, and when Sig dared to roll her eyes, I thought she was a dead woman. Instead, Fran said, 'Keep rolling your eyes. Perhaps you'll find your brain back there. But then again, it's more likely they'll fall out of that gigantic hole.' It was fantastic. And scary as hell. Over the years, she's mellowed. She doesn't normally verbally eviscerate people. Probably because people know what she expects, and only the best get to work for her."

"I, I don't know what to say. I don't suppose anyone caught it on video." She sighs.

"Nope." Harry pops the p. "Fran spent the next ten minutes dressing her down like nobody's business. She listed all the people she'd be contacting to let them know what Sig did, and can you believe that she had the temerity to ask why Fran was blacklisting her?"

"You're kidding."

"I can't make this shit up. Fran's answer: 'Let me explain this in small words so you'll understand. You will never work in this industry again. Now, get out.' The room was as quiet as a church during summer mass until Sig walked out of the conference room. Before she made it to the elevator, the room erupted. I'm talking clapping, whistling, shouting—it was like being at a Ted talk, with Fran as the keynote speaker."

"That is crazy. I'm surprised she isn't suing Sig or pressing charges or something."

"I'm sure she doesn't want the negative buzz around the game."

After a few more minutes of catching up, they promise to meet for lunch once she returns from Albany. They end the call, and Clarke thinks about what Harry told her. *Oh, to be a fly on the wall.*

Her brain gets stuck on Fran, returning to Harry's teasing remark about Fran eating her up. She remembers how talented Fran is with her lips and tongue, licking and sucking until she reduces Clarke to a screaming mess. Clarke shudders. *God.*

On Wednesday Clarke must travel to Albany to attend a series of intensives. She likes to keep up on the newest animation techniques, and some reputable, award-winning professionals are offering these classes at the university. She's excited to learn more about digital modeling, but sad it will be at least another week before she sees Fran.

Although they tried to coordinate their schedules, Clarke and Fran were unable to find the time to visit tonight or some time tomorrow. Clarke needs to finish some projects to meet her deadlines before she leaves for Albany, and Fran is deep in the hellish annual meetings with the board of directors this week. Clarke is tempted to drop by Fran's apartment on Tuesday night, but she still doesn't feel she has the right. Not unless it's scheduled. She has always abided by Fran's wishes, unwilling to push her for more time together, unwilling to give Fran an opportunity to reject her.

Nevertheless, Clarke feels her heart swell, surprised by how often Fran wants to see her. They tend to meet a couple of times each week and at least once each weekend. In fact, with Clarke's business trip, this will be the longest stretch of time since their first dinner together that they will go without seeing one another.

Clarke sighs. She doesn't know how she'll manage not seeing her for an entire week. She's always been fascinated with Fran, but since this *thing* began, she's found her thoughts often returning to Fran throughout each day. No matter what. Like now—even though she's working on creating the most exciting, innovative graphics on a project connecting a book, movie, and video game together, it doesn't keep her attention. Clarke shakes her head. She's whipped. She's not sure whether she should be concerned or not.

Noticing the time, she gets up to pack for tomorrow's trip. Although Spring is around the corner, the weather remains cold. Sweatshirts and jeans will work. Maybe a wool cap and some warm socks. It doesn't take long to get herself organized. She glances at her cell phone, tempted to call Fran. She shakes her head. If Fran wants to talk to her, she'll contact her. After shucking off her clothes and pulling on some warm pajamas, Clarke plugs in the charger and connects it to the phone. It jolts in her hand as she places it on the bedside table, and she feels her heart leap into her throat when she realizes Fran is calling her.

"Hi, Fran." Clarke sits on the edge of her bed, one hand playing with the bedspread. Her mom made it for her years ago as a present for her college dorm. It was where she kissed Julie Milton, the first girl she ever dated. It didn't last long, but she cherishes those memories of simpler times, times when she could hold hands with the woman she's dating. An involuntary smile curls her lips when she hears Fran's distinctive voice.

"Hello, Clarke. I hope I'm not calling too late. I wanted to catch you before you left for Albany. When will you be back?"

"I'll be back Sunday night." She hesitates. "Um, I'm looking forward to it, but I wish it was local."

"It could be worse. You could be flying across the country. I'm sure you'll be so busy that the time will fly by. You'll be back before you know it."

"Yeah, probably. Plus, the classes will be worth the trip. One of them is a tutorial on some of the new animation programs. It's supposed to cut down on production time and showcase natural locomotion. I just wish…" Clarke hesitates to say how she'll miss Fran. It will sound infantile and clingy. She's certain Fran doesn't want her acting that way.

"Wish what?"

"Um, that it wasn't in Albany. It's such a pain to get there. But no need to talk about that. I'm sure you have better things to occupy your mind than my transportation woes."

"Well, I'm sure everything will work out as it should. We'll touch base once you're back."

They end the call and Clarke looks around her room, feeling restless. Fran sounded disappointed when Clarke complained about traveling upstate. What Clarke wanted to say was how she wishes Fran were attending the intensive, too. How she's going to miss her. How her usual enthusiasm for these types of trips is absent because she's leaving her heart here. Shaking her head, she decides to get some sleep. She didn't say any of those things and dwelling on it won't change the fact that Fran wouldn't want to hear it. She knows Fran cares about her, but they're still far away from declaring their love for one another. In the meantime, she'll keep working toward becoming worthy of Fran's love. She's beginning to believe she might reach her goal. Someday.

***

Five days later Clarke trudges into her apartment. Who knew riding the Greyhound bus would be so tiring? It's only eight o'clock at night, but Clarke hit the ground running once she reached Albany and never stopped. She wearily places her duffel bag on the floor and opens her refrigerator, hoping food will miraculously appear so she need not order takeout. Tonight would have been a great night to stay with Fran. She always has her kitchen stocked with food, which is confusing since she eats out most of the time, but since they began spending time together, Fran has cooked for her several times, and she keeps some of Clarke's favorite snacks on hand.

Clarke had a tough time not seeing Fran's face, hearing her voice, feeling her touch. It's not as if Clarke could even call her. It's not something she does. Nor does she text Fran. At most, she might send an email about something that might have occurred on a project. She's depended on Fran to reach out to schedule each meeting. She wonders whether it's time for her to pick up the slack a bit. It's clear Fran is taking the time to see her. She might appreciate Clarke doing the same. It's something to think about.

The truth is that it takes discipline not to contact Fran. It's niggled at her, this yearning to reach out when she has a spare minute. During the week Clarke was so busy taking a series of animation classes that she was able to shelve her thoughts of Fran until she sank, exhausted, into her bed late each night. She has nothing to distract her now.

Sighing, Clarke resigns herself to ordering out and eating alone. Instead of shoving her thoughts of Fran away, though, she pulls them to the forefront. She has time tonight to devote to how she feels about the woman. To Clarke, Fran is truly larger than life. She never does anything halfway. When she decides on a course of action, she commits herself one hundred percent. Clarke has seen this happen countless times in the professional realm and to a limited extent in their relationship.

Clarke has a theory. She believes Fran is making small decisions regarding Clarke. They are adding up, building to the greatest, most treasured wish Clarke holds close to her heart. She wants Fran to commit to her completely. So far Fran has committed to spending time with Clarke, to making love to her wholeheartedly, and to demonstrating her affection when in the privacy of her home. Clarke loves every minute they share together.

Just as Clarke picks up the phone to place a food order, she hears a knock on the door. Phone in hand, Clarke looks through the peep hole to see a vision. Fran. Opening the door, Clarke doesn't try to hold back her happiness as she steps aside to let Fran pass. Hearing Fran drop her belongings on the counter, Clarke turns from locking the door to see arms reaching for her. Ravenous lips latch on, seeking out her tongue. Clarke groans at the exquisite feeling.

"Fran." Clarke's breathy whisper once the kiss breaks expresses how much she's missed the woman. That's all she has time to say before those coveted lips cover hers once more. Fran is such a wonderful kisser. Perhaps Clarke should add kissing to the list of areas where Fran commits herself fully. Certainly, she must separate it from demonstrating affection, which is an extremely broad category. Or maybe kissing is a subcategory of demonstrating affection. Maybe—

Clarke promptly loses her train of thought when Fran begins pulling off Clarke's clothes and nudging her toward the bedroom. Clarke eagerly joins in, tearing off Fran's coat, blouse, skirt, and lingerie. Soon they're on the bed, not pausing for a moment to talk or look or breathe. They just kiss, and touch, and listen, driven by days without the other, days of yearning and wanting and needing what they could not have.

Eventually they lie in a sweaty heap, allowing their hearts to slow. Fran opens her eyes to find Clarke staring at her. "Hello, Clarke," she drawls.

Clarke can do nothing but emit a chuff of pure delight. She watches as Fran smiles slightly, an impish light shining through her eyes, as deep and blue as a bottomless lake.

"Fran, you are a sight for sore eyes." She nearly melts into a pile of goo when she sees Fran's face transform into a full-fledged smile.

"So are you." Fran's soft words wrap around Clarke like a fluffy blanket. Fran lifts a finger to trace Clarke's eyebrow before moving it down her cheek. Her hand wends into Clarke's hair, pulling her forward for a languid kiss. "So are you," she whispers once more against parted lips.

Clarke snuggles into Fran's side, arm flung over her waist and leg pinning her down. Clarke doesn't want her to leave anytime soon. At least not without Clarke knowing. As she begins to fade in and out of consciousness, lulled by a hand running through her hair repeatedly, Clarke feels herself pulled out of that relaxation by softly spoken words.

"You seem to be under the mistaken assumption that you cannot contact me."

Clarke tenses, not knowing how to respond. Saying that she doesn't dare overstep the boundaries Fran has set for fear of losing her seems too revealing. Before the silence can become too uncomfortable, Clarke says, "I thought it best to wait for you to call me since you're so busy." *Not that you did. I kept checking my cell, hoping to find a message or even some notification of a missed call, but nothing.* Of course, Clarke can't say all that.

Clarke keeps her head on Fran's chest, listening to the steady heartbeat. She hears Fran's voice rumble up to her, laced with patience. "You were away on a business trip. How could I know when you would be available?"

Fran is being much too reasonable. Clarke presses her face in Fran's breasts, concentrating on the hand stroking her head.

"You don't have to wait for me to contact you, Clarke. You can suggest times to meet, too."

Lifting her head to look into Fran's eyes, Clarke nearly blurts out, *Really?*, but she refrains. It doesn't matter since Fran obviously reads Clarke's reaction.

"It's time you start contacting me when you are thinking of me, Clarke."

"Um, you'll never get any work done, then," Clarke says, ducking when she realizes what she's revealed.

Hearing Fran's soft laughter, Clarke raises her head from its tucked position in the crook of Fran's neck to look at her. Moonlight hits her white hair just right, making Clarke catch her breath. She is beautiful.

"I'll take that chance."

Clarke angles her head to observe the emotions crossing Fran's features. She appears contemplative. Clarke nods before laying her head against Fran's chest once more, thinking about what Fran said. She wants Clarke to make plans with her. That's a step forward. Hadn't she just been thinking about this before Fran arrived? It's wonderful. Thinking of all the times she stopped herself from inviting Fran to watch a movie, or take a walk in the park, or meet for coffee, or even come over, she realizes she may have misconstrued her role in this relationship. Maybe Fran has wanted her to reach out. She's disappointed in herself for being such a coward. It's amazing that Fran has put up with being the only one reaching out all these months. She's grateful. It occurs to her that this is the first time Fran has visited Clarke's home. *She must have missed me.*

After a few minutes of comfortable silence, Fran breaks it. "Now. I'm sure you are getting hungry."

Right on cue Clarke's stomach grumbles.

"We'd better feed you. You'll need as much stamina as possible." Fran rises and wraps a sheet around her lithe body.

Clarke trails behind her in a forest-green cashmere robe, a gift from Fran, ready to retrieve the telephone book to call for takeout.

Fran retraces her steps to the kitchen and picks up a bag. Clarke cocks her head in obvious question.

"Food." Fran removes the contents, the aromas tickling Clarke's nose.

Clarke grins. Fran has surprised her yet again. Showing up to see her as soon as she returned from Albany, with food, reassures her that Fran has strong feelings for her. Now that Fran has given the okay, Clarke can even contact her when she misses her. She hopes Fran's ready to hear from her every day. A finger lifting her chin reminds her that Fran is standing in her kitchen wearing a sheet. Holding delicious food. No need to miss her right now. With a grin, she leans in for a kiss. She has an appetite to sate.

Chapter Twelve

THE TRIFECTA

LOOKING AROUND HER APARTMENT one more time, Clarke straightens a throw pillow on the sofa. Her timer saves her from moving the sofa to the other side of the living room in a vain attempt to make her place look larger than it is. Fran will be here any minute. She looks around the area one more time to make sure nothing is out of place. Her apartment door opens into a small kitchen which flows into a living room and eating area. The apartment is compact, to put it nicely. Clarke shakes her head. At least she has a bathtub, not a luxury many renters can claim. Her bedroom is the largest room, big enough to allow for her to fit a queen bed, dresser, and clothing rack. It may seem to be a postage stamp in comparison to Fran's place, but it's all hers.

Moving into the kitchen, Clarke smiles when she hears the buzzer signifying that Fran has arrived. She buzzes her in and unlocks her door before taking two glasses down from her cabinet and placing them next to the wine she opened for them. Fran walks through the door, and it astounds her how, after a full day of work, she looks as if she can take on the world. Fran pivots to her, arms opening to receive Clarke's embrace. They share a few promising kisses before Clarke eases back, arms around Fran's neck. "Hello, love. I was about to start food preparations. I opened a bottle of wine to breathe, if you'd like a glass."

"That sounds lovely." Fran delivers a peck on Clarke's cheek and moves toward the counter to pour the red wine. "How was your day?"

"Good. I finished one of my projects, and I'm waiting for feedback." Clarke takes out two pieces of chicken breast and starts to cut them into squares. She can feel Fran's eyes on her, but she does her best to concentrate. Freshly cut finger isn't on tonight's menu.

Fran appears at her elbow with two filled wine glasses. Clarke takes one and they clink glasses before taking their first sips. "*The Cerulean Dragon* project?"

"Why do you sound so surprised?" She peers at Fran.

"It's a complex animation, particularly with the characters changing into different types of animals and the corresponding power fluctuations. I figured that would take several more months." She reaches out, caressing Clarke's cheek. "My reaction is not toward your abilities. I've made it no secret that I believe you are a gifted animator."

Clarke lights up, treasuring Fran's compliment. "Thanks. I get it. It usually would take a lot longer, but I'm using some new processes that cut down on the steps. I'm able to upload handmade drawings and connect them to motion capture and motion matching. They fill in the gaps, so to speak."

"Did you learn that in Albany?"

"Yup. It was a really good conference. I also applied a new technique after reading an article on invisibility." Clarke looks up and grins when she sees Fran's curiosity. "Scientists have been researching how to use silk coated with gold to bend or reflect certain energy wavelengths around them. In effect, it works like a shield, hiding whatever the material surrounds and allowing the observer to see what is behind the shielded object. Like in Harry Potter, they can hide what's cloaked. Scientists are hoping to use it for medical means, but the military is also experimenting."

"How are you adapting that for a video game?" Fran's pensive look prompts Clarke to expand on her idea.

"The best sci-fi and fantasy games incorporate science and nature since they ring true and provide footholds into reality. I created a character who finds a way to make an invisibility cloak using this research. I'm hoping the project lead will like the idea." Clarke has put a ton of work into the narrative for this storyline, and she thinks the cerebral quality she's integrated into the story will attract more players.

"You have a wonderful mind, Clarke. If the lead doesn't like the idea, we can incorporate it into one of our games. One way or another, we'll make sure your ideas are seen." The way Fran speaks about it reassures Clarke that her ideas are worthy. That what she has to say and how she thinks are important. It's a heady feeling.

After finishing with the chicken, Clarke washes her hands and takes out the rest of the ingredients she needs to cook a chicken stir fry. This is the first time she'll be cooking for Fran, and she's decided to fall back on a dish she knows like the back of her hand. She has plenty of recipes she wants to try, but tonight is not the night for experimenting. She washes the vegetables and places them on a cutting board. The orange, red, and yellow peppers she found at the farmer's market yesterday look beautiful and will provide a bright pop to the stir fry.

"May I help with anything?" Fran is leaning against the other counter, one arm over her stomach and her elbow resting on it as she holds her wine glass. Clarke loves how relaxed she is. She's business casual today, which tells Clarke she didn't have any meetings with investors or board members. She's wearing a red cashmere sweater and a pair of charcoal-gray wool slacks. A chunky, silver-toned bead necklace rests on her clavicle, matching earrings complementing her long neck.

Reminding herself that she can explore that lovely neck with her lips after dinner, Clarke swallows down her lascivious thoughts to answer. "Sure. Can you cut the onion and press the garlic for me?"

Fran nods her head, and Clarke places a clean cutting board, knife, and a garlic press on the counter. It surprised Clarke to learn that Fran loves to prepare her own meals. Although she often dines at restaurants, it turns out that whenever she has time, she prefers to cook her food. Clarke doesn't mind since she's tasted the scrumptious results several times.

Once she finishes cutting the rest of the ingredients, Clarke washes her hands and retrieves her apron for cooking. She doesn't want to ruin her clothes with cooking oil splatters. As she concentrates on cooking the stir fry, Fran slides her strong arms under the apron and wraps them around Clarke's abdomen. Clarke shivers as her body flushes, a bolt of arousal rushing through her. She's embarrassed by how easily Fran affects her. They stand entwined for several minutes, enjoying the embrace.

Fran nibbles her neck while hands wander over Clarke's belly and thighs, stalling on her hips. Taking a deep breath, Clarke rests her head on Fran's shoulder, humming when hands slide up her torso, cupping her breasts. It's amazing how good Fran's hands feel, how magical her fingers are, how hot her breath is. Clarke becomes lost in sensory overload, immersed in the vanilla notes of Fran's shampoo and the solid body wrapped around her. Fran's lips slide up the column of her neck before she nibbles an earlobe, her fingers rolling tight nipples. Clarke feels herself toeing the edge, ready to explode as the current stimulation overlays her memory of past encounters. Her eyes flutter shut, and she takes a deep breath to slow down her heartbeat. She feels like she's running a marathon, her body alight with sensation. Fran continues to play with her breasts, rolling and pulling on the sensitive tips while her other hand moves down to cup Clarke between her legs. Clarke's moan is long and deep. She wants more.

A shrill whistle breaks through Clarke's haze of desire. It takes her a moment to open her eyes, and even longer to understand what is occurring. She stares in disbelief at the smoking ruin formerly known as their meal. "Shit!" Clarke removes the wok from the stove and dumps it in the sink, turning on the faucet to spray water over it. With smoke billowing from the sink, she opens the small window to the left of the stove, ignoring the brisk wind. Finding a chair, she climbs up to silence the alarm. The sudden silence is a relief to her abused ears. She hops off the chair and slumps into it, one hand covering her eyes.

"Well. Not much of a cook, are you?"

Fran's teasing is unwelcome, and Clarke scowls. "I was distracted." Clarke huffs as she supports her head on one hand. Most of the smoke has dissipated. She sits back and crosses her arms over her chest. What a disaster.

"Don't fret." Fran smirks at her, not at all upset that they have nothing to eat.

Clarke gets up and looks in the sink. She wonders whether it would be best to throw it out instead of trying to clean it. The night is a bust, as far as she's concerned. It isn't like she has extra food stowed in the refrigerator. Now what is she supposed to do? She braces herself against the sink, head dropped as she tries to rally.

A warm hand slides down her spine. "Clarke, please don't be upset. I'm sorry I distracted you while you were cooking. We still have the chicken. Do you have any pasta?"

Straightening up, Clarke turns her head, looking into concerned eyes. "I have some ziti, but I don't think I have any sauce."

"We'll figure it out. Do you mind if I rummage around to see what you have?"

"No, make yourself at home." Clarke looks at the chicken, already cut up into cubes. She supposes she can rub them with salt, pepper, and garlic powder and cook them in oil. She pulls out the drawer at the bottom of the stove to remove a skillet.

"You have the ingredients for an alfredo sauce. Will that suit you?" Fran holds a block of parmesan and a stick of butter in one hand, and a quart of cream in the other one.

Nodding, Clarke gets to work on the chicken while Fran stands next to her. Fran places a large pot of water on the backburner to boil for the pasta before measuring out what she needs for the sauce in a small pot. Clarke's embarrassment lessens as the pleasurable food aromas replace the stench of burning vegetables. Twenty minutes later they sit down to eat, and Clarke is amazed at how easily they recovered from the ruined meal. Dinner is delicious, and Fran flirts with her while they enjoy their meal. The way Fran's eyes make promises. Clarke can do nothing but release any lingering perturbation.

Once they finish, Fran insists on helping her clean up. Although she's tempted to leave the mess until the next day, she doesn't want to imagine how hard it will be to save the burned wok. Better to take care of it tonight. Clarke places the leftover food into containers, glad to see she'll have a tasty lunch tomorrow. When she turns to deal with the wok, she realizes that Fran is washing it. "Oh, you don't have to do that."

"I most certainly do. I caused the mishap. The least I can do is clean it. Plus, look, it's coming off easier than I thought it would." She holds up the pan for Clarke to see before continuing to scrub the burned remains off. They finish cleaning the kitchen and sit down on the sofa, refilled wine glasses in their hands. They chat about whatever enters their minds, the ebb and flow of the conversation acting as a balm to her frayed nerves. The earlier mishap wasn't that horrible, and who could really blame her for losing her concentration with Fran's magic hands roaming over her body? They were able to course-correct, and the night is getting better by the moment.

Much later, Clarke covers Fran's body with her own on the sofa, kissing her with passionate intent. She has big plans, which include making love to Fran in several areas of her small apartment. Needing to leverage herself to explore more skin, Clarke blindly moves her hands to support herself on either side of Fran's body. Only her left hand finds no purchase, and she topples off the furniture with a whoosh.

Lying on the floor a bit dazed, Clarke hears rich laughter ring through the room. Opening her eyes, she rolls onto her stomach with a groan and props herself on her elbows, her eyebrows rising and mouth dropping as she witnesses Fran laughing so hard that she's holding both arms across her stomach. If her eyebrows were able to fly off her head, this would be the moment.

"Ouch." Clarke feels mortified. Fran is laughing at her clumsiness. She hangs her head, fighting tears. Talk about killing the mood. Fran only laughs harder.

"Oh, Clarke, really." Fran's wheezing gasps are a sight to see, but that doesn't placate Clarke's bruised pride.

Rising in slow motion, Clarke plunks herself on the couch, thoroughly put out. In different circumstances, she might find the entire situation amusing. Her Rico Suave impression failed spectacularly, and if their roles were reversed, she admits to herself that she might be the one fighting to catch her breath after guffawing for several minutes. The only saving grace is how gorgeous Fran looks as she lets loose. It's as if years of stress are rolling off her shoulders, giving her a carefree, joyful appearance. She's never heard Fran laugh like this. It's addictive.

"Well, that was fun." Clarke rises. "Be right back." She enters the bathroom, and once she closes the door, she stares at herself in the mirror. With her bright eyes, flushed cheeks, and swollen lips, she hardly recognizes herself. Taking a few deep breaths and exhaling slowly, Clark calms down enough to let go of her mortification. After using the bathroom and freshening up, Clarke detours to the kitchen to grab the wine bottle before rejoining Fran on the couch. She fills up both their glasses with the remainder of the malbec wine they opened after dinner.

"I hope I didn't hurt your feelings." Fran looks contrite, her eyes dark.

"It's fine. My pride is a bit bruised, but I probably would have laughed my ass off, too."

"That would be a shame since I happen to love your ass." Fran wiggles her eyebrows.

The action is so unusual coming from Fran that Clarke giggles. Her mood lifts, and she holds out her glass. "To loving an ass."

Fran looks at her suspiciously before smirking. "Well, I've been called worse." She clinks their glasses together and takes a sip from it.

They settle down to work while listening to the silky strands of jazz. Although Clarke tries not to brood over the mishaps during tonight's date, she's disappointed. Her inability to cook a delicious meal or even stay on the damn couch during a promising kissing session has shaken her fragile self-esteem. She's surprised Fran hasn't left.

Clarke tries to concentrate, but since the night isn't progressing the way she'd imagined, and she's a glutton for punishment, she racks her brain for an idea to get them back on track. That's when she gets a bright idea. "Wanna play strip poker?"

"Strip poker?" Fran enunciates the words slowly, a predatory smile crawling over her face. "Are you sure, Clarke?" She slowly trails her eyes over Clarke's body.

Okay, well, sure, Clarke's wearing a dress while Fran's pantsuit bespeaks more bargaining chips, but Clarke used to play poker every week for years. How bad can it be? Less than an hour later Clarke's able to answer that ridiculous question. She can hardly look at that smirking face as she removes her panties—her final betting piece. Fran remains fully clothed. Well, this is a hat trick of embarrassing incidents. If she played hockey, others would celebrate these regrettably unforgettable performances.

Well, shit. Hearing Fran clear her throat, Clarke pouts, not daring to look up. *Why did I think it was a good idea to invite Fran over for dinner?*

"You are adorable."

Clarke presses her lips together after hearing Fran's murmured words. She doesn't want to feel better. The entire night has been a catastrophe. She stares at her hands, clasped demurely on her lap, waiting for Fran to tell her that she's going home.

"It is during such times I find you irresistible. Let me prove it to you."

Fran's offer makes all the misfires seem like tiny hiccups. Perhaps she hasn't ruined the night. Looking up, Clarke sees an outstretched hand and a tender smile. How can she resist? She takes the proffered hand and allows Fran to lead her into the bedroom. During the time it took to enter, Clarke lets go of her mopey mood and running monologue of the many ways she destroyed their date. After all, how can she hold on to that when her arms are filled with the love of her life? It's as simple as that.

Chapter Thirteen

SCHEDULING TIME TOGETHER

WORKING ON THE LAPTOP gifted to her months ago is a constant reminder of how stepping up to protect Fran, even when scared, has paid off a thousand-fold. Clarke wishes she could dismiss how afraid she was, but the truth is she's still afraid. Afraid Fran will come to her senses and drop her without looking back. Afraid of doing or saying something to hasten that eventuality. Afraid she'll admit how in love she is with Fran, only to have Fran laugh it off or worse, pity her.

Clarke knows she should trust Fran a bit more at this point. They've been together for six months, and she's even spent time with Fran's daughter. That wouldn't happen if this were merely a fling. In fact, Fran has encouraged her to ask for time together instead of relying on Fran to always reach out.

Hearing her email inbox signal a new message, Clarke saves her work and clicks over. Seeing Fran's schedule, sent by her assistant, Clarke grins. This must be Fran's way of prompting Clarke to be more active with suggesting when they can spend time together. Reviewing the schedule, Clarke notices a week blocked off in June for vacation. Clarke doesn't remember Fran mentioning a trip. She wonders whether she can ask about it. Deciding she's not brave enough to question Fran's schedule yet, Clarke settles for sending an email to her, requesting her presence on Friday at her apartment for dinner. Clarke wants to cook for her. Maybe even not burn it this time.

Nothing too fancy, of course. Clarke is thinking steak and salad. A home-cooked meal will serve as a pleasant change of pace from all the restaurant food. The only time they didn't eat at a restaurant was when Fran's daughter was home for Spring break and last month's debacle. Clarke wants to start spending more time with Fran in private. She wants Fran to be able to relax around her, to let Clarke in more.

Fran's reply is quick and affirmative. Clarke smiles. Then she frowns. That's three days away. Clarke drums her fingers on the desk. She won't be able to last that long without seeing her. She sighs in resignation. What's the worst that could happen?

Rejection, derision, sarcasm, coldness, dismissal. *Right.*

But she misses the woman. And Fran has given Clarke permission to contact her.

Realizing she's whining to herself; Clarke decides to bite the proverbial bullet and contact Fran again tonight. Maybe not by telephone. That may be too nerve-wracking. Texting will work.

Having made the decision, Clarke is able to buckle down and concentrate on a smaller but lucrative project she received last week. The company approved her proposals yesterday, and she's in the middle of creating the main character, a bad-ass woman under overgrown bangs and dowdy clothes—a diamond in the rough. This is her favorite part of the process, breathing life into characters she creates from pencil drawings to 2D and 3D graphics.

Several hours later, Clarke stretches her hands over her head, turning her head to either side to loosen taut muscles. Looking at the clock, Clarke exhales loudly. *Where did the day go?* After a few moments of psyching herself up, Clarke sends a text to Fran: *Do you want me to bring you dinner?*

Fran's schedule shows she's been outside the office most of the day for meetings. Normally, that means Fran will stay late to catch up on paperwork. Hearing her cell vibrate, Clarke reads, *Yes. 9:00p.m. Surprise me.* Clarke grins. She had no idea it would be this easy. This communication thing might not be that bad.

An hour later Clarke strides into Brightman-Cook and stops for a visitor's pass. She's pleasantly surprised to receive a permanent pass, barely able to mask her reaction. As she rides the elevator, memories bombard her. She hasn't entered this building in nearly seven years. Clarke takes a deep breath to calm her nerves. She's envisioned countless fantasies involving this elevator and Fran.

As she walks toward the Haboob Software reception area, Clarke wonders whether everyone has left for home. No one seems to be around. A moment later Clarke passes the pit where she used to have a desk and stops in the doorway of Fran's office to feast her eyes on the woman.

Fran sits in her chair, spectacles low on her nose as she reviews what looks like storyboards. A fitted, ivory silk blouse with a deep V-neck encases Fran's torso, the color emphasizing her signature hairstyle. A chunky pearl necklace invites Clarke to linger over a delicate neckline, and the ebony pencil skirt allows for a wonderful view of toned legs ending in Jimmy Choo's. She only dresses up this much when meeting with the board of directors. It's Clarke's lucky day. She feels breathless. After several moments of visualizing those legs wrapped around her waist as they make love, Clarke's brought back to reality by acerbic words.

"Do you intend to make me starve, or are you coming in?" Fran's eyes continue to bounce over the storyboards. She has one leg crossed over the other, her toe moving lazily in a circle.

Clarke's face heats up as she realizes Fran caught her ogling. The lightness in Fran's eyes when she looks up and the upturn of her lips calm Clarke's mortification enough for her to respond. "Sorry. I was just admiring the view." Clarke shrugs as she crosses to the small table on the far side of the room. Placing dinner on it, Clarke firmly instructs herself to behave before turning toward Fran.

And promptly forgets the admonition as she's kissed within an inch of her life. Clarke moans, extremely aroused and a bit disoriented. Strong fingers support her lower back as Fran continues to stroke Clarke's tongue with erotic lingual caresses. "Ung," Clarke groans as Fran's hand cradles her head, angling it so she can explore Clarke's mouth more thoroughly.

When Fran releases her lips, Clarke has a tough time opening her eyes or closing her mouth. She can feel saliva coating her lips, can taste Fran on her tongue, can feel one hand still tangled in her hair and the other one rubbing circles on her back as Clarke tries to recover her wits. Finally opening her eyes, Clarke witnesses a tender look on Fran's face. Clarke gasps. "Oh, I, thank you."

"Hmm. My pleasure." Fran leans forward again to deliver a chaste kiss. "Wine?" Fran asks before crossing the room to a small refrigerator.

"Yes." Clarke unpacks their shrimp-topped salads, using the dishware already on the table. Fran appears beside her with a bottle of pinot grigio.

Before sitting down to eat, Clarke pulls Fran into a hug, nuzzling behind one ear. It feels so wonderful to hold her. She sighs, feeling contentment steal over her. With a shy smile, Clarke disengages and takes a seat.

They make quick work of the food and wine while discussing their day. Fran relates the astounding incompetence surrounding her is astounding. "At least Harry didn't behave as if he'd received a lobotomy over the weekend."

The way Fran complains about her staff always entertains Clarke. She has the best talent around, yet she makes them sound like first-year interns. *Like I used to be.* Clarke shares her latest project and is pleasantly surprised to receive several insightful ideas. Clarke supposes she shouldn't be since Fran has always made sure to know what's occurring in their industry. She may not create videos anymore, but she keeps her finger on the industry's pulse to know the latest advances. Clarke can't help but wonder whether she will ever be able to keep up with Fran. She frowns at the thought. How can she ever be worthy if she's always running to keep up?

Fran clears her throat, causing Clarke to shake herself from such debilitating thoughts. "Elaine will be out of school next month. She'll be staying with me for most of the summer." Fran pauses to sip her wine. "She'd like to spend more time with you, if you are amenable."

Clarke grins. "I'd love to. We can catch a movie, or a show, or take a walk in the park, or…" Clarke stops when she sees the expression on Fran's face. "What?"

"I—I," Fran stutters before taking a deep breath and letting it out. "Yes. That will be lovely. She'll love it." Fran nods her head definitively.

"You're welcome to join us, of course," Clarke says slowly while trying to figure out Fran's reaction. "Anytime, anywhere." Clarke stops again at Fran's reaction. "Fran?"

Clarke becomes nervous, as she sees tears lurking in the corners of Fran's eyes. Her eyes shimmer as she directs a tremulous smile at Clarke. "Thank you."

Not knowing what to do, Clarke leaps out of her chair to clean up. Fran seems a bit stunned when Clarke takes their dishes into the small kitchen area. Upon her return to Fran's office, she notices Fran standing next to the window, lost in thought as she runs her finger over the top of the wine glass.

Clarke locks the door before rejoining Fran, silently basking in the city lights and Fran's aura. "Do you need to return to work?" Fran continues to look out the window after she asks her question, but her finger motion has abated. She's listening. It takes a moment, but Clarke realizes Fran is watching her through the window reflection.

"No, I have everything I need on the laptop." Clarke has no desire to leave Fran. All that she has to look forward to tonight is an empty apartment and a lonely bed.

"I have a bit more to do before I can leave. You can work here." With the matter settled, Fran returns to her desk.

"Okay." Clarke feels a bubble of happiness well up from her belly. Fran wants her to stay. Clarke settles on a comfortable chair in the far corner. She loses herself in the assignment, breathing life into the new animation while incorporating the list of requests she received from the project manager. Every so often she lifts her head to gaze at Fran. It seems surreal to be sitting in her office late at night as they both work on separate projects. It feels wonderful.

It reminds her of how well they worked together years ago. It reminds her of how she panicked when she realized she 'd developed feelings for Fran, feelings she knew would not be returned. Back then she was a wet-behind-the-ears intern. She received instructions and executed them, and each night she reviewed her textbooks to prepare for the next day. When she realized how besotted she was, she decided to leave as soon as her internship ended. It was unusual for an intern not to seek fulltime employment, but not unheard of. Her need to escape eclipsed her career ambitions. Fran was kind enough to offer a recommendation. It surprised her. Clarke was under the impression that Fran hadn't really noticed her, not more than any other grunt bent over a computer for countless hours each day. Yet the recommendation made it clear that Fran noticed everything. Clarke shivered.

After another hour of work, Clarke is satisfied with the clothing designs she's created for the main character's opening sequence. She looks up to find azure eyes devouring her and shivers. "I'm sorry. Was I keeping you here?" Clarke asks.

"Not at all." She continues to study Clarke before saying, "Come here." It's a command, and Clarke jumps up to do Fran's bidding.

A few paces bring Clarke in front of Fran who grasps her hands firmly. Tilting her head Fran says, "I'm glad you contacted me, Clarke. You've made my evening much better. It amazes me how having you near helps me." She looks around the office before focusing on Clarke once more. "Even when you worked for me, you always made everything more manageable." Fran's murmured words thrill Clarke.

Lifting Clarke's hand to kiss her knuckles, Fran continues. "It wasn't until after you left that I really began to understand what you meant to me." She stands from her chair, moving well into

Clarke's space. "If you only knew how often I've imagined having you here with me, like this."

Startled by the desire shining brightly in Fran's eyes, Clarke can only think of one thing. She leans forward oh-so-slowly to brush her lips against hers. Hearing her moan, Clarke deepens the kiss while continuing to hold her hands with a tight grasp.

When the kiss ends, Fran whispers, "I tried to forget you. I tried to move on." She breaks their hold and frames Clarke's face with trembling fingers. "You thought you were just another intern walking through a revolving door, but it's not true." Their lips brush lightly, meshing erotically before Fran pulls back just enough to see Clarke's face. "Don't make me wait anymore, Clarke. Make me yours. Here."

Clarke's eyes widen. She's never been the aggressor in their sex life. She's never initiated their lovemaking, but Jesus, she has so many fantasies involving Fran and this room from which to choose. Clarke pulls Fran to her and slams their lips together. She unbuttons Fran's blouse as she licks the inside of her mouth repeatedly. The noises Fran makes drive Clarke to distraction. Clarke's fingers shake as she parts the blouse, fingers skating over creamy skin. Gently pushing Fran against the desk, Clarke replaces her fingers with her mouth, making her way down a heaving chest to lick the spaces between each rib.

"God." Fran clings to Clarke's shoulders, fingers digging in, as she squirms under Clarke's onslaught. Her exclamation encourages Clarke to keep going, to take what she wants, to make Fran hers.

As cliché as it may seem, Clarke has always wanted to make Fran lose control on the desk. Clarke smiles widely as her fingers squeeze two lace-encased nipples. Fran's breathless gasp is an effective aphrodisiac. She feels powerful.

Tonguing Fran's bellybutton while unzipping her skirt, Clarke slides her fingers downward, taking skirt, hosiery, and panties with them. Lifting each foot as she kisses toned calves, Clarke removes all items quickly before moving her head upward once more. "Do you like this?" Clarke asks as she widens Fran's shaking legs and begins sucking on an inner thigh. She can smell Fran's arousal, can see how wet she is. Licking a stream of liquid, Clarke stops short of touching its origin as she looks up.

Fran's eyes are wide and dark as they watch Clarke. Mouth slightly open as her fingers flex restlessly on Clarke's upper back, she is the epitome of wantonness.

"Do you?" Clarke asks again, louder.

Fran nods as she gulps. Clarke rewards her by licking hard on her clitoris. Fran shrieks and bucks. Rising, Clarke ignores the sound of discontent as she grasps her lover's hips and lifts her onto the desk. Stepping between Fran's legs, Clarke takes control of Fran's mouth as she makes short work of the bra. Now Fran is naked and exactly where Clarke wants her. Palming Fran's heaving breasts, Clarke pulls on tight nipples repeatedly as she thrusts her tongue into Fran's mouth again and again.

Sensing that Fran is close, Clarke breaks the kiss and whispers, "Do you know how many times I've fantasized about you here? Of taking you, of making you scream?" Hearing Fran's whimper, Clarke sucks on her collarbone before licking up the neck column to an ear. "I've had you on every inch of this floor." Fran moans. "Against the windows, in your chair. But the best fantasies, those I can never forget, are when you are on this desk." Clarke gently lowers Fran so she is reclining, legs spread for her.

Gazing at Fran, flushed and ready, Clarke burns the image into her memory. Bending down, Clarke begins licking and sucking, nibbling and blowing on every inch of Fran's sex. Clarke holds Fran's hips in place, taking immense pleasure in wringing responses out of her. As Fran arches yet again, trying to place Clarke's tongue where she wants it, Clarke inserts three fingers into the slippery channel and sucks on the sensitive bundles of nerves. Fran screams, her body spasming as her release takes over. Clarke pulls Fran's gyrating body closer to her mouth, determined to make the orgasm last. Continuing to thrust her fingers, Clarke twists them, rubbing hard. Fran screeches as another orgasm crashes over her.

Feeling Fran's body go limp, Clarke stills her fingers and licks gently over the area. Looking up, she sees Fran's eyes closed as she takes deep breaths through her nose. Clarke withdraws her fingers and licks them ravenously. Her body hums with need, but she doesn't want to break the spell which has fallen over them—this stillness, this feeling of magic, and power, and love which blankets them. Clarke smiles at how right it feels.

Fran's eyes open as she offers a lazy smile. "You've worn me out, Clarke." Sitting up slowly, Fran's eyebrow hitches as she peruses Clarke's attire. "In a hurry, were we?"

"I didn't care to be distracted from loving you," Clarke admits as she shifts from foot to foot. They are remarkably close, so close Clarke can feel heat roiling off Fran's beautiful body. She is hard-pressed not to take Fran again. She feels her pulse jump at the thought.

Arms wrap around Clarke's waist, pulling her as close as possible to Fran's beautiful body. Clarke's attention is diverted by legs wrapping along the back of her thighs and a hand guiding her face toward waiting lips. "Oh," Clarke says before she loses herself once more to Fran's siren call.

"I want to see you," Fran whispers throatily. Nimble fingers quickly divest her of her clothing while Fran speaks softly. "I've never allowed anyone to take control before. Certainly not here. For me, sex has always been a source of power." Fran is now standing next to the desk as she unzips Clarke's slacks. Clarke kicks off her shoes and steps out of her pants without breaking their gaze.

"Perhaps I never trusted anyone enough." Fran turns Clarke so she is facing the desk. She presses her body against Clarke's back sensually as she places little kisses on the nape of Clarke's neck and across flexing shoulders. Clarke's body trembles so much that she must lean forward to brace her hands against the desk. Fran continues to kiss her back softly. "But I trust you, Clarke. I know you would never seek to hurt me."

Clarke agrees wholeheartedly. "Never. I'd rather hurt myself."

"I know." Emotion stains Fran's voice.

When she feels Fran move away, Clarke starts to turn around.

"No. Stay exactly where you are."

Clarke stays but whimpers her need. Soon, though, she feels Fran's body heat on her back once more and sighs. Fran places a cool hand between her shoulder blades and pushes her forward.

"Spread your legs, darling."

Clarke is quick to comply. She feels Fran's other hand squeezing her ass as lips glide down her spine. When Fran's hand slides into her wetness, Clarke's moans become long and loud. Clarke pushes backward as Fran drives two fingers into her. Clarke's chest becomes level with the desk as her ass pushes upward to meet Fran's rhythm.

"You are gorgeous, Clarke. So giving, so willing." Fran speeds up her strokes, thrusting harder.

Her passionate words compete with Clarke's thundering heartbeats. She can do nothing but moan.

"Have you thought of this, Clarke? Of me fucking you here, like this?" Fran's voice is louder, stronger, demanding an answer.

Clarke can only moan louder. Fran inserts another finger and quickens her strokes. Clarke feels the building of an enormous orgasm.

"Do you trust me, Clarke?"

"With my life," Clarke declares in a shaky voice. "With my heart," she whispers. She is so close she can taste it. Clarke begins to protest when Fran withdraws her fingers, then squeaks as she feels something pressing against her opening. *A dildo? Has she been planning this?* Clarke's body trembles at the thought.

Fran grasps Clarke's hips firmly before entering the younger woman. "—Ung. Oh my god." Clarke groans. "Fran, you feel incredible." She wails when the toy hits a particularly sensitive spot. She can hear Fran panting as she thrusts, pulling out nearly completely before pushing forward once more. Each stroke hits Clarke perfectly. She feels so filled that she cannot stop herself from begging. The room fills with pants and grunts, a symphony of love.

"Fran, please don't stop. Don't ever stop. Just like that. You feel so good." Clarke mumbles a litany of such words, loving how completely Fran is taking her. Perspiration pools on her lower back, as she listens to the sounds their bodies make as they pound together.

Fran has sped up, and Clarke can tell she's close to another orgasm. This excites Clarke so much that she begins to lose control. "Fran, I'm going to, I can't stop it, I—Fran." Clarke screams, overwhelmed by wave after wave of ecstasy. She hears Fran's shouts of satisfaction as their bodies slap together for several more moments. Finding herself flattened against the desk with Fran plastered against her, Clarke hums her pleasure. She has no desire to get up. Her body is exhausted. Turning her head to the side, she twists so she can capture Fran's lips. "I love you."

It's possible she blacks out for a few moments. When she opens her eyes, she realizes that Fran has pulled out of her and is rubbing Clarke's back soothingly.

When their eyes meet, Fran says, "I love you, Clarke."

Clarke feels her exhaustion swept away by joy. Pushing off the desk, Clarke turns to embrace Fran. She laughs, unable to contain her happiness. Smiling brightly, Clarke gazes into glistening eyes. "Thank you, Fran. Thank you."

"For what?"

"For loving me." Kissing Fran tenderly, Clarke feels as if her entire world has changed. She supposes it has.

They clean up in silence. It's not necessarily uncomfortable, but it is full.

Once they are both clothed and their belongings packed, Fran calls for the car. Touching Clarke's cheek gently, Fran asks, "Come home with me, Clarke?"

Clarke nods. There's no place she'd rather be. And it's as simple as that.

Chapter Fourteen

GROWING PAINS

SINCE THE WORLD TURNED on its axis when they declared their mutual love, Clarke has found herself spending much more time with Fran. Every day they communicate somehow. It's as if the floodgates opened once Clarke sent her first invitation to Fran to have dinner in her home. Now it's common for them to email, text, and phone the other daily. Clarke loves it.

With this change, Fran has become more relaxed, going as far as to crack jokes at the most unexpected times. Clarke loves how quick-witted Fran is. She feels privileged to experience this side of her since she's known to be the consummate professional outside of her home. It amazes her how Fran can still surprise her, even after being with her for seven months. Seven glorious months.

Clarke sweeps her gaze across her apartment one more time, wanting this evening to be perfect. The first time Clarke made dinner for Fran at her apartment, it became a comedy of errors. To Clarke's chagrin, Fran often teases her about that night, but it wasn't her fault. The woman is a menace. It turned out the night became better. Much better.

Clarke sings under her breath as she removes dinner from the oven. She's cooked meals for Fran several times over the last couple of months and twice for Elaine. Tonight, though, it's just the two of them.

Most of their meals are at Fran's home—quite the change from eating at restaurants. Once they began texting and calling one another, though, it seemed natural to share more meals together in a private setting. On many occasions, Clarke has arrived at Fran's home directly after work. After eating, they tend to settle into the den where Clarke works on her projects and Fran completes Haboob Software work. It's all rather homey and comfortable. When their workload is light, they push it off until after dinner, preferring to use the time to kiss. And what a kisser Fran is.

Never in the past has Clarke spent hours making out. Every part of Fran intoxicates her. She is drunk on Fran. Amazingly, Fran seems just as enthralled.

Hearing the intercom, she presses the button to buzz Fran inside the apartment building while crossing to the door to leave it ajar.

She stirs the rice, listening for Fran to arrive. When she hears the door close, she smiles before turning around. "Perfect timing."

Fran quirks an eyebrow haughtily as her eyes rove over Clarke's attire, who stands still for the inspection. She's wearing True Religion jeans she splurged on and a gauzy flower-printed blouse. Clarke watches Fran's eyes darken with appreciation, and she shivers as goosebumps break out on her arms. Fran's hold on her no longer surprises her. Nor does her visceral reaction to her focused gazes.

"Darling." Sometimes Clarke wonders how Fran's able to say so much with one word. Like now. That one word drips affection and attraction, relief and desire. Coupled with the look, it causes Clarke to feel weak and powerful.

"What concoction are you springing on me tonight?" Fran strides toward Clarke, and before she can answer, luscious lips demand her attention.

Clarke swallows Fran's appreciative moan, as arms wrap around her waist. With reluctance, Clarke ends the kiss after indulging for a few moments and steps back, shooting a stern look at Fran. "Oh, no you don't. I spent hours slaving over a hot stove for you." Clarke's cheeky admonishment isn't true, but based on this greeting, Clarke recognizes she'll want to eat to keep up with Fran's libido. "Sit down, sweetheart." As soon as Fran sits down, Clarke dishes out their meal.

Fran's smirk lets Clarke know she isn't insulted. They eat their halibut in relative silence while holding each other's gazes and brushing fingers every so often. Clarke feels warmth suffuse her. She loves this woman so much. Although they do not voice such feelings often, Clarke knows their lack of verbal expression does not mean they aren't present. Clarke can feel their connection thrumming, its feeling akin to the rushing of her blood.

After dinner, they settle on the couch to stream a movie. They choose an action movie, delighting in studying the special effects and pronouncing whether they are well-done. As the end credits roll, Fran turns to her.

"Have you arranged for vacation time at the end of the month?" Fran asks out of nowhere.

"Why would I do that?" Clarke doesn't understand why Fran levels a glare at her.

"Don't be ridiculous. You've had my schedule for months." She stares at Clarke as if she has three heads—three hollow heads.

"Was I asleep when you asked me to go on vacation with you?"

"What are you implying?" Fran responds in such a cold voice that Clarke swears she's getting frostbite.

"I'm not implying anything." Clarke crosses her arms. "I'm saying that this is the first time you've mentioned anything about our going on vacation together." She doesn't understand how the hell she's supposed to know what Fran wants.

"If you were so confused, why didn't you ask?"

"Why didn't you?" Clarke shoots back.

After a loaded silence, Fran looks away. Clarke notices her stained cheeks and feels vindicated. "I am asking you now." Fran maintains an even voice, but Clarke can see how fast her pulse is racing.

Although Clarke recognizes this is as close as she'll get to Fran admitting she may have made a mistake, she is feeling contrary. "What if I don't have enough vacation time left?" When Fran's head swings around with a critical look, Clarke shrinks back.

"When did you go on vacation?" Fran demands, her eyes narrowed.

"In January, to visit my parents." Under the weight of Fran's stare, Clarke expands. "It was just for a couple of days."

"Why is it you never speak of them?"

Clarke doesn't want to talk about her parents. She shrugs. "So, where is this vacation I was supposed to pencil in?" Clarke tries not to grimace at how falsely bright her voice sounds. Although Fran stares hard at her, she tries to maintain the stare without blinking. She blinks.

"Clarke."

Fran's deep voice shouldn't turn Clarke on, but it does. With a sigh, Clarke recognizes that Fran won't let this go. "We haven't had the best relationship. It's been rocky for a while." Clarke looks out the window. She really doesn't want to discuss this.

"How long is a while?" Fran asks.

Shaking her head like a petulant child, Clarke looks away. She feels a hand slide over her forearm and worm inward. Clarke relents, allowing Fran to take her hand.

"Years." Clarke sighs. "We had a falling out right after I left Haboob Software."

"Right after you left me."

Fran's correction fills Clarke with dismay. "Fran." Clarke feels a thousand years old, certainly too tired to discuss this again. She tries to pull her hand away, but Fran does not permit it.

"Why did you have a falling out?"

"I was not myself. They thought once I left Haboob Software, I would be the old Clarke again. Instead, I began working on a bunch of projects and I was, I don't know, despondent. I just didn't have the energy to pretend everything was fine." Clarke begins to trace an imaginary pattern on her leg. "I was unhappy. Lonely. I missed— Life was not unfolding as I wished."

"And they noticed?"

Clarke snorts. "Oh, yes. They noticed. And they figured out what was really troubling me. They said some horrible things, some hurtful, unforgivable things. So, I stopped talking to them for a couple of years. If it weren't for Natalie getting married—she's my older sister—I still might not be talking to them." Clarke glances at Fran, noting her contemplative look. "Our relationship has never recovered."

The room is quiet as they digest what Clarke has said. Lost in the memories, Clarke startles when Fran says, "What was the falling out about?"

Clarke shakes her head. She doesn't want to tell Fran it was about her.

"Clarke?"

Clarke sets her jaw and tucks her head. Gentle fingers lift her chin, turning her face toward the older woman.

"Tell me." Fran's soft command prompts Clarke to admit the truth.

"It was about you."

Fran gasps, shock clearly showing on her face. "Me?"

"I missed you." Clarke doesn't know how else to explain. She had missed Fran desperately.

"Why didn't you contact me?"

"Oh, sure. I'm sure you would have been receptive." Clarke shakes her head. "Didn't we have this conversation several months ago?" Clarke cracks a smile. They really are hopeless. It's a wonder they ever got together.

Fran glares, but there's little heat attached. In direct contrast to the look, Fran's voice is velvety. "Come on vacation with me, Clarke."

"Okay." Silence. "Where?" The glower Clarke receives is genuine. Clarke grins. "How am I supposed to pack?" She tilts her head and bats her eyes.

With a theatrical sigh, Fran waves her hand in a careless motion. "The weather is comparable to here. Bring a bathing suit and a passport. That's all you'll get, so don't try."

"Right." Clarke nods docilely. Fran rolls her eyes.

***

"You're eating dinner with Fran now?" This is how Harry starts their conversation. Clarke hasn't even sat down yet. It's a week before Fran is to whisk her away somewhere, and Clarke is extremely excited. Once settled, Clarke takes a deep breath. She discussed this eventuality with Fran the other morning at breakfast after seeing Fran's smile and her own laughing face peering at her from Page Six.

They were surprised not to have found themselves in the newspaper more often. Clarke could only remember two other occasions. With this picture, though, they could expect more attention. It told the world that they were close. Everyone wants to know how close.

Anticipating Harry would ask, Clarke looked to Fran for guidance on how to handle his questions. She was no help at all. Fran raised an eyebrow and directed Clarke to say what she wished.

Clarke shoots a bright smile at Harry. "It's great to see you, Harry. How are you? Getting ready for the next big project?"

Harry scowls as he points a finger at Clarke. "Don't you try to change the subject. How long has this been going on?"

"It was just dinner, Harry. No big deal." Of course, it is a very big deal. Three nights ago, neither had wanted to cook so they had eaten at the Essex House. Clarke didn't have much experience with French cuisine, but all the food tasted heavenly.

The photograph reflects two happy women sharing a joke. Since the rest of the world believes Fran does not know how to smile, never mind laugh, everyone has been plaguing Clarke with questions. It's easy to brush off colleagues. Not so much a friend.

"No big deal?" Harry's voice rises. "She was smiling. I can count on my left hand the number of times I've seen her smile." He raises his hand dramatically and wiggles his fingers. "Spill it, Cap."

Seeing Harry's determined expression, Clarke concedes. "Okay. Yeah. We've been keeping in touch since the Sassy debacle. You knew that already." Clarke picks up a menu and begins to study the lunch entrees. Hearing crickets chirping, Clarke realizes Harry is not going to let this go. Lowering her menu enough to see him, Clarke gazes into disbelieving eyes. "What?"

"Since Sassy? You've been meeting since Sassy?" Harry's choked voice makes her want to laugh. It makes her want to run away.

Did I say that? Clarke wonders. *How did he get that? Shit!*

"Um, yes?" Clarke fidgets under his stare. "Okay, okay. We have been spending some time together. I—I"

"Oh my god! Are you two—don't tell me…" Harry's voice fades as he slouches in his chair. "Are you two involved?" His whispered words sound strangled, as if they were torn from him.

Clarke has a decision to make. She can't help but believe she can trust him. They are friends and he has stuck by Fran through thick and thin. She owes him the truth. Clarke nods slowly, then watches Harry with concern as his face loses color. Scooting forward in her chair, Clarke leans on the table and asks with an urgent voice, "Harry? Are you okay?"

"Am I, am I okay?" Harry shakes his head as if he has just received the mother of all punches right on his nose. He pauses to sip some water from the sweating goblet before refocusing on Clarke. "How serious is this?"

"Well, I spend time with her daughter, we have the key to each other's apartments, we're going on vacation next week, and we spend every spare moment together. So, yeah, it's pretty serious." Clarke grins suddenly. "I love her. As impossible as it sounds."

Harry stares at her as if he has never seen her before. "You love her?"

"I do. I don't think I could go a day without talking to her." Clarke shrugs. "She's everything to me. It's amazing I was able to function without her in my life for so long."

"I see." Before Harry can say more, the server arrives to take their order. When Harry looks at her again, he seems calmer. "I should have realized something was happening. Fran has been different for a while. Not smiling and laughing, of course, but more tolerant, calmer." He sips his drink. Running his fingers up and down the glass methodically while his eyes sport a faraway look, he seems to be having an inner debate. "Against all odds you've tamed our lioness. She's quite a complex lady." Harry pins Clarke with a gaze. "And so, it would seem, are you."

Clarke scrunches her eyebrows, not sure what to say. She's never seen Harry like this. "Well, I'd like to think I am more than two-dimensional."

"And so you are. She always saw something in you. She was much more patient. I could never figure out why."

"Gee, thanks."

Harry smirks. Lifting his glass, he toasts her. "To the complexities in life. May you both never run out of things to discover about each other." They clink glasses with mirroring smiles.

"Does your family know?" Harry asks as they munch their salads.

"No. Although with us appearing in the newspapers, it's only a matter of time." Clarke glumly spears a spinach leaf.

"They won't approve, I take it." Harry pushes his empty salad plate away and sits back.

"No. Not at all." Clarke peers at Harry. "It's not the same-sex part. It's the fact that I am with Fran. They won't understand."

"You may want to tell them before the press does it for you." Clarke knows he's right. "So. Vacation, huh? I can't remember the last time she took one. I knew something was fishy. I thought she was going with her daughter, but this is so much juicier." Harry rubs his hands together in anticipation. "Where are you going?"

"I have no idea." At Harry's skeptical look, she elaborates. "I'm serious. All she will tell me is that the weather is comparable to here and to bring a bathing suit. And my passport."

"Tropical. You're going somewhere tropical. Jesus. She's getting romantic. For you." Harry tilts his head, considering Clarke for several moments. "You'll need some clothes. Don't look at me like that. Flannels and jeans won't cut it. Tell me you have more than that."

"I do. Of course, I do. I have the best T-shirts and khakis." She giggles at his look of horror. "Stop it. I'm a grown woman. I own several shirts without words on them and nice slacks. Even a few skirts and dresses. I'll be fine. I promise."

Harry's forehead smooths out, and he nods. "I'll have to take your word for it. At least until I see the pictures. I expect you to text me a slew of them, preferably when you're both in bathing suits."

"You wish." Glad the conversation wasn't as painful as she feared, Clarke takes another bite of her ravioli.

"She's been working like a horse to get everything done."

"I know." Clarke frowns. "We've hardly seen each other. The other night was last minute. It will be worth it, though. An entire week alone with no work." Clarke waves a finger at Harry. "I'm counting on you to hold down the fort. No emergencies, no crises. She needs to relax." Clarke stares at Harry sternly. She's dead serious.

"I'll do my best, Cap." Harry's reply is cordial. Clarke's glad he's not taking offense. "Besides, it's not every day La Silvetti falls in love and takes a vacation. Lord knows I've never seen the two together. And now, knowing what I know and reviewing how she's acted over the last seven months, I can't help but wonder whether I've ever really seen her in love before." Harry rubs his chin.

"Well, the feeling is entirely mutual. All I want to do is make her happy."

"Keep doing what you're doing. It's all she needs."

Clarke smiles gratefully. After a not-too-uncomfortable silence, they move on to other subjects. She fills him in on her newest project, taking the opportunity to pick his brain for ideas when she finds out he's worked with the company in the past.

Before parting ways, Harry kisses her cheek and holds her at arm's length. "You really are something else, Cap."

Clarke sees admiration in his eyes and cannot stop the wide smile that takes over her face. "She is, too. If you only knew."

"I'm starting to, Cap. I'm starting to." He waves before stepping toward a parked taxi and opening the passenger door. "Have a great trip." His words, called through the open window, light her up. She practically vibrates with excitement.

Instead of returning to the apartment, Clarke decides to head toward Fran's home. Fran has urged her to do so, insisting it doesn't matter whether she is present for Clarke to be there. Since Elaine's visiting friends in Virginia for the week, Clarke can get some work done while she waits for Fran to return home. Happiness wells up within her chest.

Entering the quiet apartment, Clarke decides to set up in the home office and work on a small face animation project that's due at the end of the week. Like Fran, Clarke is under the gun to finish all her assignments so nothing will interrupt their vacation.

Looking around for scrap paper to use while reviewing what steps she needs to complete, Clarke opens the top desk drawer. Inside Clarke sees a framed photograph of them. Picking it up, she recognizes it as the picture taken of them outside of the Essex House and smiles. Fran really is a romantic. Tracing Fran's face with a finger, Clarke shivers in remembrance of that night and Fran's outrageous flirting. She places the photograph prominently on the desk with a smile.

Finding what she needs, Clarke gets back to work. When she finds a breaking point, she decides to go to bed. Fran won't mind, and she wants to get some sleep so she can power through and finish the project tomorrow. Taking a quick shower, Clarke decides to sleep in the nude. Thoughts of how Fran might awaken her swirl through her tired mind, and she falls asleep with high hopes.

Several hours later Clarke wakes up to the feel of a silky arm sliding over her waist as delicate lips rest briefly on her neck. "Darling," Fran murmurs.

Clarke runs her hand down Fran's forearm and rests it on top of hers. "Hello, love." Clarke moves her head back to rest on Fran's shoulder to provide better access. "How was your day?"

"Better now."

Clarke turns around in the comfortable bed. Pulling Fran closer Clarke winds her arms around her small waist and kisses her slowly.

"Mmm. Much better." Fran's sexy hum fills the space between them.

"I'm glad you're home." Clarke snuggles into Fran's chest, squeezing her and delivering a kiss to her sternum before falling back to sleep, content that all is right with the world. Her world. The one that revolves around Fran.

Chapter Fifteen

LETTING THE WORLD KNOW

THE OCEAN AIR IS heavy with brine, the feel coating Clarke's arms. She leans against the balcony railing, listening to the waves lapping at the shore. This trip is a dream come true; a dream she didn't realize she'd wanted. The hotel, located on the Gros Islet at St. Lucia, is exclusive. Beautiful. Luxurious. So much like Fran. Their suite reflects opulence and wealth. Fran has spared no expense. She seems to delight in Clarke's reactions to each new experience. Clarke sighs, feeling all her worries fall away. They needed this week together. A week to connect and relax without the normal stresses dogging their heels.

"Ready to go?" a breathy voice asks. Turning toward Fran with a nod and a ready smile, Clarke's smile turns into an 'O,' much like some cartoon character's face might make when viewing the most incredible sight one could never anticipate. "See something you like?" Fran's smoky voice surrounds Clarke, who has forgotten how to do anything other than stare at Fran, slack jawed.

"Wow." She tries to swallow, to get some saliva in her mouth. "You look, you look, oh my god. I am the most fortunate woman alive." Clarke shakes her head, at a loss to find the right words. "Breathtaking, Fran. Incredible."

She feels like a simpleton, but she can't find the words to describe how beautiful Fran looks. It's not merely her outfit, although she looks delicious in the loose ivory linen dress she's wearing. It's the inner glow and the easy smile that entice Clarke. She's never seen Fran look this at ease.

Fran's soft laughter lets Clarke off the hook. She feels strong fingers grasp her hand to pull her gently toward the door. "Let's go before your eyes swallow me up. It would be a shame to miss such a glorious night. Let's eat. I'm ravenous." Fran stares at Clarke with a salacious stare. "And you'll need it."

I'm so lucky.

They hold hands as they walk to the waterfront restaurant. The night is balmy and well-lit, thanks to the full moon. Once they arrive, they're led to an outdoor table on the back deck. Clarke looks around in wonder. The moonlight bounces off of the water's surface, claiming her attention. She loves listening to the waves as they pound against the sand, the susurration of pebbles and shells filling the air seconds later as the tide ebbs. The cyclical sounds soothe her as she smells the salty brine. Taking a deep breath, she exhales all the stress she has stored in her shoulders. It's silly to feel insecure when the love of her life has brought her to this magical place.

A server arrives, and after placing the order for drinks and appetizers, Fran takes Clarke's hand. They sit in companionable silence, enjoying the ambiance. On their bleached-wood table is a small hurricane lamp, producing enough light for them to read the menus. Twinkly lights wrap around the deck fencing, adding a bit of magic. The sea air invigorates her, and by the time the server returns with their drinks and appetizers, she's ready to order her entrée.

The lobster bisque and stuffed mushrooms are delicious and pair well with the wine Fran chose. It's all Clarke can do not to moan as she tastes each delectable bite. By the time they start on their entrées, Clarke's tastebuds are dancing in her mouth, well-pleased by the food selections. She enjoys the catch of the day, grilled with fresh vegetables, while Fran indulges in a surf and turf combination. The food is decadent, and Clarke feels spoiled by the attentive servers. After dinner, they stroll along the promenade, in no hurry to be anywhere except in one another's company.

"This is wonderful." Clarke links arms with Fran and leans in to deliver a quick kiss to her cheek. "I can't tell you how happy I am to be here with you."

"Me, too. I've never subscribed to the notion of taking vacations when I needed a break, but with you, the idea is much more palatable. Enjoyable, even."

Elbowing her, Clarke shoots her an incredulous look. "Well, that's high praise. You should stop your gushing before I get a big head."

"I'm saving that for when we're alone. I do have a reputation of being a heartless devil to uphold." Fran's flip words serve as a reminder of how unfair people can be to high-level businesswomen. Fran always takes it in stride, but Clarke is learning to see behind the veneer she dons for the world. Although Fran acts as if all the insults that she receives roll off her back like water on a duck, she's not impervious to the hateful language. Clarke recognizes the gift Fran has given her by opening her heart and allowing herself to be vulnerable. She'll do everything she can to make sure Fran doesn't regret it.

The next morning soft lips awaken Clarke, trailing down her chest as hands knead her breasts. Clarke moans, overwhelmed by a wave of arousal. "Fran?" Clarke squeaks as she looks down her torso to see a white bob moving while a tongue delves into her bellybutton.

"Were you expecting someone else, Clarke?" Fran drawls with a smirk before sucking on a tender spot at Clarke's abdomen. Clarke wiggles at the sensation, whimpering when Fran squeezes her nipples, twisting and rolling them, as her mouth attacks her belly.

Clarke lets out a shaky breath as she attempts to not thrust her pelvis upward. She clings to Fran's shoulders, massaging them while Fran continues her loving assault. "Jesus, Fran!" Clarke pants when she licks the hollow of her hipbone. Fran looks up, a devilish look on her face, a lock of hair falling across one eye. That does not hide the raised eyebrows or flashing teeth, as she smiles fully.

Widening her legs so Fran can rest comfortably between them, Clarke mewls as Fran takes a stiff nipple into her mouth, humming while she sucks forcefully. Clarke can no longer control her body's movements, focusing only on how good Fran makes her feel. Not wanting to let her have all the fun, Clarke runs her hands down Fran's back and takes a firm hold of slim hips. Clarke pulls Fran toward one leg, and she doesn't hesitate to slide on to it while switching her attention to the other breast.

"You have such lovely breasts, Clarke." Fran licks one while cooing compliments. Her talented tongue laves Clarke's breast with long strokes. "You are a very beautiful woman." She pauses her feasting to capture Clarke's eyes. "I love how you make me feel."

Pleasure swells within Clarke. Fran isn't one for romantic words, but when she speaks in this way, Clarke knows she's completely serious. Clarke doesn't try to stop the smile that bursts from within.

Reaching down while her other hand rests on the small of Fran's back, Clarke's fingers slide through copious moisture into her center with ease. Fran begins to thrust on to Clarke's fingers as her slim fingers fill Clarke. Clarke lifts a leg to wrap around Fran's waist while grinding her palm against Fran's clitoris. Listening to her gasp and moan feeds into Clarke's responses. Moments before they climax, Clarke hears Fran mutter, "I don't think I'll ever get enough of you."

"I'm yours for as long as you want." Clarke speaks from the heart, her body tightening as a forceful orgasm grips her. She slams her eyes closed and screeches her pleasure. Fran's yell of triumph mingles with her voice as they move in tandem. Their bodies undulate against each other, elongating the feeling of ecstasy. All she can hear are their attempts to catch their breath, and with eyes still closed, Clarke doesn't try to keep her happiness in check. She chuckles, her voice hoarse.

"Hmm?" Fran licks a bead of sweat between Clarke's breasts.

"I love waking up with you." Clarke cups Fran's face, leaning down to deliver a brief kiss. She runs her fingers through sweaty locks as her heartbeat begins to slow. They reposition themselves so that Clarke can enjoy the sound of Fran's heartbeat under her ear. It lulls her in and out of consciousness. When the rumbling of Fran's stomach awakens her, she knows it's time to rise for breakfast.

Fran delivers a thorough, devastating kiss before rising from the bed and extending a hand toward Clarke. "Shower?" Clarke takes her hand and follows Fran's siren call without hesitation.

Waking up to Fran each day, showering together, making love. This vacation has opened her eyes to how easy and wonderful sharing her life with Fran is. She hopes Fran feels the same way. Awakening in the middle of the night, Clarke gazes at Fran's relaxed visage and wonders whether she's dreaming. She grabs her cell phone and types out a small poem.

Dream of me softly like blues of the sky reflecting in your eye
Dream of me purely like whites of the cloud rising up proud
Dream of me passionately like reds at the start flagging your heart
Dream of me true as I look at you; free as the soul—yours is my goal
Dream of me fragrantly like greens grown in spring, like the love I bring
Dream of me sweetly like shades of the day cavorting in play
Dream of me constantly as I do of you—if only you knew
Dream of me
Dream of me
Dream of me

Rereading it, Clarke smiles. *I guess I'll call it 'Dream of Me.'* Now that she's written the poem, she feels lethargy overtake her. With one more look at Fran, Clarke closes her eyes, hoping she'll find her love waiting for her.

They spend the next day at the spa and the evening at another exclusive restaurant, making love until they fall asleep well-sated. Once they awaken on their third morning to bright sunlight filtering through their bedroom suite, they rent a yacht and others cater to them like royalty while they sunbathe, frolic with the dolphins, and discuss whatever enters their minds.

"Clarke, have you told anyone about our relationship?"

"Just Harry." Clarke continues to apply suntan lotion on Fran's pale shoulders. She doesn't want Fran to get a sunburn. Rubbing in the white cream evenly, she doesn't hesitate to kiss the shell of Fran's ear before returning to her task.

"No one else? Your family? Friends?"

"No one else." Clarke places the lotion down next to her chair and studies Fran's back to make sure she got every piece of delectable skin.

Fran turns her head to deliver a questioning look. "Why?"

"I didn't know whether that would be okay with you, I suppose." Clarke shrugs. "It doesn't bother me, Fran." Clarke wonders at the look on Fran's face.

"Are you ashamed to be with me, Clarke?" Fran turns more in her lounge chair to face Clarke squarely.

"Ashamed? Of you?" Clarke hears her voice rise. She lets loose a nervous laugh. "Fran, that's ridiculous. I love you. I-I'm the one." Clarke points to herself. "I'm not worthy here. I'm woefully less than what you deserve. I can never..." Clarke spreads her hands helplessly. "...hope to give you what you need, I—"

"I don't expect you to provide for me, Clarke." Fran's lip curls up, her derisive sneer an unwelcome clash with the halcyon day in the sun. It feels as if the clouds are gathering over their heads, ready to drench Clarke with Fran's contempt. "That's not what I need from you." Fran stares at Clarke. "I've let you into my life. Don't you understand what that means?"

"I know you are a very private person." Clarke speaks slowly, searching for the right words to placate Fran. Her mind works overtime to figure out why she seems hurt. "I feel privileged to be with you. I'm grateful for any time we spend together."

"Maybe that's the problem." Fran gazes across the ocean, her face as still as the water. "Many can tell you that it's no privilege to be with me—"

"Then they don't know you," Clarke interjects hotly. Fran places a placating hand on Clarke's arm, stopping her from saying more.

"Clarke, you don't need to be of the same economic standing. You don't need to be at the same place in your career. You don't need to be anyone other than who you are. I don't love you for who you might become one day. I certainly don't want you to feel grateful or that it's some great privilege to be with me." Fran takes Clarke's hands into hers, looking down at them before continuing.

"I believe I have loved you since the day you walked into my office, that day when you had no idea who I was." Fran looks up, eyes sparkling. "The next day when you appeared, wearing a flannel, a Def Leppard shirt and Converse high tops cinched it." Fran smirks before her face takes on a serious expression. "I was bereft when you left me. I nearly tracked you down." Fran runs her fingers over Clarke's shaking hands. "But I thought it would be better to let you go. You deserved better than what I could offer you. I had no idea you harbored similar feelings."

Shaking her head, Clarke starts to object, but Fran places a finger over her lips to silence her.

"I want you to understand that if anyone should feel grateful, it is me. You came back into my life and gave me a second chance. And every moment we have shared together has made me feel as if I am the privileged one in this relationship." One hand cups Clarke's cheek. "I am not ashamed to be seen with you. I want you in my life. Tell whomever you wish." Fran smiles at Clarke's shocked expression and kisses Clarke's nose. "Clear?" Clarke nods dumbly.

Fran takes the bottle of lotion and turns Clarke toward the ocean view. Moments pass as the motion of the yacht and Fran's strong hands massaging her back lull her into a relaxed state. "What did they say to you?" Fran asks softly. Clarke tilts her head in question. "Your parents. What did they say that was so terrible you stopped talking to them?"

Clarke sighs. Thinking about it still hurts, yet she knows Fran has the right to know, particularly since her parents will learn of their relationship soon. "Where to begin..." Clarke muses over how much to reveal. "Well, they were shocked and disappointed with me. They did not want to accept how inconsolable I was, particularly since they felt that I was working too many hours while interning for you. They believed there must be something seriously wrong with me to miss a person who probably couldn't remember my name." Clarke stops recounting when she hears Fran suck in a deep breath.

"I'm sorry, Fran. They only knew how hard I worked and how high your expectations were. They didn't know you the way I did. They didn't see what I saw." Clarke places her hand on one of Fran's, currently resting on her shoulder. "You mesmerized me." Turning, Clarke looks into upset eyes. "You still do. I honestly don't know how to live without you." Clarke laughs humorlessly. "I was doing a lousy job before you invited me to dinner last November." Clarke smiles. "And I've been the happiest woman on this planet since then." Clarke relaxes when she sees the answering smile in Fran's eyes.

"So, you chose me when you didn't even have me."

"Damn right. And now that we're together, you'll never get rid of me."

"Well. That happens to coincide with my plans perfectly." Fran's flirting always makes Clarke smile. She loves when Fran is playful.

"You have plans?" Clarke raises her eyebrows, tilting her head in question.

"Oh, yes. Big plans, Clarke. Just you wait." Fran shoots her a mysterious look and a knowing smile before reclining on her chair and closing her eyes.

"Tease." Clarke wants to know what Fran's alluding to. Right now.

Fran opens her eyes. "I assure you, I am entirely serious." With a smirk, she closes her eyes and places sunglasses daintily onto her nose. Conversation over.

Clarke knows how futile it will be to try to get more information out of her. With a sigh of defeat, she leans back in her chair and closes her eyes. A hand finds hers, squeezing it before letting go. Clarke can't help but smile.

Three more days of lavish accommodations and carefree relaxation pass by like sand through her fingers. "Fran, we're going to have to do this again." She gazes at Fran as they sip wine on the balcony.

"We certainly will. I intend to work on that list of places you've never visited." Fran's lips quirk in amusement at the dumbfounded look Clarke sports. "What are your plans for your birthday?"

"My birthday?" Clarke says in surprise. Fran rolls her eyes. "Right. Um. My parents are insisting on visiting."

"Really. Perhaps we can all meet for dinner on that night." Fran stares at Clarke, waiting for her response.

Not a question, Clarke thinks in a daze. "Do you think that's a good idea? They won't have much time to get used to the idea, and I don't want you to feel uncomfortable." Clarke stops when Fran laughs mockingly.

"Me? Uncomfortable? Really, Clarke. Are you forgetting who I am? How others react to me?" Clarke can tell Fran is not going to let this go. "Clarke," she says with a gentler voice. "I want to celebrate your birthday with you. I promise to play nice. Besides, don't you think it's time we met?"

"It's not you I'm worried about," Clarke says morosely. "I do want to spend my birthday with you. I do. I just…" Clarke shrugs. "They can be tough."

"Tell me, Clarke. Are they staying in a hotel?" At Clarke's nod, Fran continues. "Good. No matter how they behave, no matter what words they hurl in our direction, at the end of the night you will be in my arms. Keep that in mind. I know I will," Fran says drily.

Clarke can't help but chuckle. "Okay." Silence. "Where are we going?" Fran lifts an eyebrow. "Right." *She's a romantic.* Fran smirks. *Did I say that out loud?*

Chapter Sixteen

DANCING WITH THE DEVIL

TELLING HER PARENTS ABOUT Fran is as horrible as Clarke anticipated. Her parents must have learned from their last falling out, however, since they ask to call back after they have processed the information that Clarke has been dating Fran for eight months. Not knowing what to say, Clarke agrees.

She putters around her apartment, knowing she won't be able to concentrate on her work projects. When Fran invites her over for dinner, she decides a change of scenery might help her shake off the funk she's slipped into. She really doesn't feel up to anything more than eating and sleeping.

They eat in relative silence. It soothes Clarke's frazzled nerves. If she hadn't felt the absolute need to see Fran, to feel those addictive arms encircling her for at least a few moments, she would have avoided coming over. Instead, Clarke's mind keeps rehashing her parents' clipped words and loud silence on the line when she told them that she's dating Fran. She picks at her food, not hungry. Normally she loves this meal, chicken piccata. Tonight, though, nothing interests her.

Looking up from her plate, Clarke sees concern reflected in beloved blue eyes. She tries to smile, but she fears it turns out to be more of a grimace. Pressing her lips together, Clarke sighs. "Maybe I should go. I'm not particularly good company tonight."

"Nonsense. I'm glad you're here." Fran's firm reply warms her heart.

Clarke stares at her plate, trying to psych herself up to eat at least some of the tasty meal. A hand covers hers, and Clarke glances up once more as Fran pulls her out of the chair.

"Am I correct in assuming you are done eating?"

"Yes. I'm sorry, Fran."

Fran holds Clarke's hand and leads her to the den. "No apologies. Everyone has bad days, even you." Gently pushing Clarke on the couch, Fran sits down next to her and wraps her up in strong arms. "Do you care to discuss what's bothering you?" Fran runs soothing fingers through her hair.

"Not really." Clarke sighs. What can she say? Her parents suck. She hates the thought of not spending her birthday with the three people she loves the most. Clarke feels strong fingers massaging her skull and closes her eyes in bliss.

"All right. Why don't you try to put it from your mind then?"

"I'll try." If Fran continues what she's doing, she just might be able to.

"I'll help you." Fran delivers light kisses along Clarke's jaw.

Clarke's body melts under such loving ministrations. One delicate hand strokes her cheek while the other talented hand continues to rub away the stress trapped at the top of her head. Clarke sighs again.

Pliant lips find hers, lightly brushing once, twice, before barely pressing against Clarke's lips. As if they have all the time in the world, Fran moves her lips slowly, mesmerizing Clarke. She swallows reflexively as fingers pull her closer and Fran's hot mouth breathes life back into her. Opening her own mouth, Clarke groans her pleasure. Breathing through her nose, Clarke touches her tongue to Fran's and nearly smiles as Fran shivers in response.

Their tongues frolic for endless minutes, hours, days, while Fran's fingers continue to massage and worship Clarke's head. Although a dull throbbing between Clarke's thighs began as soon as their lips met, Fran takes care not to escalate their kisses into a precursor for making love. Clarke reads Fran's intentions clearly and loves the woman even more for such treatment. Whenever their kisses become too probing, too passionate, Fran pulls back and begins the process of gentle kissing once again.

Taking Fran's cues, Clarke explores every inch of Fran's mouth. She becomes lost in the texture of her tongue, the pressure of her lips, and the taste of her breath. She revels in the openness Fran demonstrates, the willingness to push away her own needs while catering to Clarke's need for comfort.

Much later Clarke can't help but wonder how she's come to be lying on her back with Fran resting on top of her. Running her fingers through Fran's iconic hair, Clarke opens her eyes. Maybe life doesn't suck after all. "Thank you." Fran kisses the hollow of her throat in answer.

They pass the rest of the evening watching comedies before turning in early. Clarke worries that Fran will be upset, but she isn't in the mood to make love. Once they are in bed with the lights turned off, Fran spoons Clarke, her arm holding her close.

"I love you, Clarke. Tomorrow will be a better day." Fran kisses her on the cheek.

Settling a hand on Fran's forearm, Clarke closes her eyes. She knows as long as she wakes up in Fran's arms, everything will be all right.

Clarke doesn't hear from her parents for a week. She began to believe that Fran would have Clarke all to herself for her birthday, but her parents finally called to confirm their travel plans. The conversation was painfully brief.

"Are we to understand that we will be having dinner with that woman on your birthday?" Clarke's father asked.

"Yes. Please don't make this hard, Dad."

"We'll see you next week."

Her parents flew in this morning, and Clarke is a wreck. She wants to continue to enjoy her birthday. It began so wonderfully. Fran awakened her with kisses and flowers, breakfast in bed, and passionate lovemaking. All the while Fran made sure to tell Clarke how beautiful she is, how much she adores her, how she loves waking up with Clarke in her arms.

That is something Clarke will never tire of—finding Fran next to her in the morning. Ever since their vacation, Clarke awakens to find herself wrapped up in Fran's arms. It makes mornings the best part of those days. Although Clarke does not always sleep at Fran's house, she relishes the times they are together. Fran has offered to come over to Clarke's apartment several times, but she finds she prefers Fran's home. In many ways, Clarke feels she is growing out of her apartment. It seems juvenile and empty, just a place for her to sleep.

When Fran asked her to stay over the night before, Clarke felt joy suffuse her. Clarke knows she is staying over tonight, too, and she cannot help but feel grounded by that knowledge.

Not that it's helping her to calm down right now. Clarke looks out the window once more before resuming her pacing in the den. Fran will be back soon to change before they leave to meet her parents. Clarke offered to pick them up, but her parents declined. She still has no idea where they are going. Fran's assistant related all the details to her parents, and Clarke hasn't spoken to them, other than to confirm they made it into the city safely.

Smoothing her hands over her black wrap dress, one of the few dresses she owns, Clarke takes several deep breaths. Tonight will be fine. Everyone will be painfully polite. They will chit-chat, eat, and leave. Clarke will see her parents at some point tomorrow or the next day. Then they will fly back to their lives while Clarke continues to be with Fran. Simple.

Just as much as Clarke is dreading this dinner, she is anticipating spending time with Fran. It is becoming harder and harder to stay away even for a night. If she had her wish, Fran would ask her to move in with her. She finds it hard not to drop hints about it, but Clarke has promised herself to allow Fran to set the pace of their relationship. So far, this strategy has yielded wonderful results. She intends to stick to what works. Fran wanting to meet her parents, even knowing the hostility they feel, is a big step. Clarke loves her for not shying away.

Hearing footsteps on the hardwood floor, Clarke moves toward Fran. They meet in the hallway. Fran's face lights up, her arms opening wide as she reaches Clarke.

"Hello, birthday girl." Fran wraps her arms loosely around Clarke's neck. Fran pulls her in for a gentle hug, one hand tangling through Clarke's dark curls while the other one makes soothing circles on her upper back. "Just remember that at the end of the evening, you will be coming home with me."

Staring into Fran's eyes, Clarke asks, "Do you promise?" She feels her throat closing, and she tries to swallow several times. Perspiration forms on her brow. She doesn't understand why she is so afraid. Their relationship is solid.

Fran pulls back to look into Clarke's eyes. "I promise, Clarke. Nothing they say will change my feelings for you."

Clarke nods. She dissolves into a sweet kiss that is much too short before Fran steps back.

"I won't be long." She watches Fran ascend the stairs with a sigh.

When they step out of the town car an hour later, Clarke cannot help but lose her breath. They are in front of one of the most exclusive restaurants in Manhattan. Clarke once mentioned it in passing to Fran, teasing that even she would have a challenging time getting a table. Fran responded that the chef was a hack, and anyway, if she had any desire to dine there, which she emphatically did not, she would.

"I thought you didn't want to eat here?"

"But you do." The twinkle in Fran's eye relates her pleasure with surprising Clarke. "Shall we?"

Once inside, Clarke sees her parents standing off to the side. Walking over to them, Clarke kisses them both on the cheek before stepping back toward Fran. "Mom, Dad, this is Fran. Fran, this is my dad, John, and my mom, Maureen." Clarke watches her father stick out a hand to shake. Fran raises an eyebrow and leans in to deliver air kisses. She does the same to Clarke's mother. "Right, shall we?" Clarke extends her hand toward the maître d' who is patiently waiting for them to follow. Clarke indicates for her parents to precede her, feeling Fran's hand on her lower back.

"I love you," Fran whispers as she gently nudges Clarke forward. Clarke cannot help but smile.

After ordering champagne and appetizers, Fran asks questions about her parents' trip, leading the conversation like a pro. It's easy for Clarke to forget how charming she can be during social situations. Any time they can spend together they hoard jealously, choosing not to socialize or share those moments with anyone other than Fran's daughter.

Clarke has a feeling they'll be socializing more often, though. Some of her friends have questioned the increasing number of pictures showing up on Page Six. Now that Fran has given her blessing, Clarke wants to tell the world how lucky she is to be with such an extraordinary woman.

"I see you have our daughter wrapped around your dainty finger."

Clarke whips her head around to stare at her father, unable to believe she heard him correctly. "Dad, what are you doing?"

"I'm guarding your interests. Someone has to. She's had you spinning your wheels since you first met her." He glares at Fran. "But you know that already, don't you? You think it's all fun and games to seduce a much younger person, someone who adores you. Does it make you feel powerful, Fran?" The sneer on his face shocks Clarke.

"Of course it does. She is magnificent in every way. I love seeing her blossom under my ministrations." Fran answers in a matter-of-fact voice, except for the final word. That word she massages with a suggestive lilt.

Did she just say that? Clarke can't think. "Fran, please don't." When Fran dismisses her whispered plea with a glance, she feels as if Fran slapped her across the face.

"How dare you! Do you know what you've put this family through?" Clarke's mother grips her water glass tightly enough that Clarke fears it will break. The outrage is clear in her voice.

"Nonsense. You chose to pass judgment on Clarke's heart. With one so young and idealistic, how could you expect her to listen to you?" Fran doesn't seem to care that she's making the situation worse by making Clarke sound like some young, naïve girl. She seems to enjoy toying with her parents, and Clarke feels a lead ball form in her stomach. She knows she needs to do something to stop Fran from digging into her business persona of the heartless devil.

"Now wait a minute…" Clarke begins, but stops, not knowing what to say but needing to stick up for herself. Fran casts a baleful eye at Clarke, clearly telling her to be quiet.

"She has continued to listen to her heart, and now she has tendered it into my care. You might want to respect that choice." Fran sips her wine as if she has just finished discussing the weather.

"Don't you patronize us," Clarke's father hisses. "She may not be able to see past your single-minded desire to possess her, but we can. She's not an object you can use and then throw away like yesterday's trash. She's our daughter, and she deserves better."

"Regardless of my intentions, it is her decision to make." Fran turns to Clarke. "Would you care to dance, Clarke?"

"Would I, would I care to dance?" Clarke knows she sounds like a parrot by repeating Fran's words, but she feels a bit dazed. Maybe getting Fran away from her parents for a bit might help. "Um, yes." Clarke's eyes widen at the imperious look she receives and rises quickly to take the proffered hand.

Once they reach the dance floor, she turns to Fran and wordlessly accepts her left hand, placing her own on Fran's shoulder. She feels Fran's other hand rest on her back. Following Fran's lead, she notices quickly how she purposefully uses her hips to indicate their direction. Throughout the sensual dance, Fran keeps their eyes locked through pure force of will. By the end of the first song, Fran has Clarke pinned to her intimately with her hand burning Clarke's lower back, effectively holding her in place. She's shocked by Fran's behavior.

She sees something in Fran's eyes, something that makes her uncomfortable. Is it a flash of superiority? Triumph? Clarke's having trouble grasping what's occurring. Searching those blue eyes, she recognizes the cold condescension she used to witness daily so many years ago. She doesn't understand. As they sway to the final vestiges of the song, she views her parents' faces. They seem upset as Fran pulls Clarke in even more and dips her head toward Clarke's neck to kiss it. Clarke shudders.

This display is so unlike Fran. She has always acted cordial yet reserved when they have appeared in public. Clarke's stomach churns. Is this affectionate display some type of powerplay on Fran's part? A show to prove to Clarke's parents that she can do whatever she wishes to Clarke? She tries to pull back but feels Fran push on her lower back to keep her in place. "Fran?" Clarke asks, confusion clearly conveyed through her voice.

"Clarke." Fran kisses her neck again.

Clarke stiffens. Pulling her head back so she can peer into Fran's eyes, she sees a gleam of satisfaction as Fran stares at their table. "Let's go sit down." Clarke stops dancing.

"Not yet."

"I'm getting uncomfortable. Can't we, can't we just try to get through dinner?"

Fran ignores Clarke's plea. "Clarke. Are you telling me that you don't want to dance with me?" Her raised eyebrows and frosty voice warn Clarke to deny that extremely farfetched suggestion.

"N-no. I love being in your arms. I just, it's just that, shouldn't we go back to the table soon?" Clarke feels like a pawn in some silent chess game or the dubious prize of a strategic war of wills. She knows that her parents do not stand a chance.

She doesn't mind the fact that Fran so obviously has set out to demonstrate her hold on Clarke. It is how Fran seems to enjoy flaunting such power and how she's taking it for granted that is upsetting her. "Come on, Fran. You've proven your point."

"What point exactly, Clarke?" Fran's mild voice doesn't fool Clarke. She's had enough.

"That I'm yours. I'm sure they've gotten it."

Fran sniffs. "I have no idea what you are prattling on about." With that she lets go of Clarke's back, running her hand over Clarke's ass before walking toward the table regally. Clarke trails behind her.

They sit in silence as Clarke struggles with the situation. Her father seems to be grinding his teeth, and her mother's face is flushed with anger. Fran sits as if she were meditating in front of a serene lake. Clarke decides to break the silence. "Um, so, how long will you be in town?"

"Is that all you have to say, young lady?" her father asks, practically spitting out the question.

"What—what do you mean?"

"How can you allow her to paw you like that in public? Do you have no shame? No self-worth? She's treating you like her personal plaything, and you're letting her!" Her father's voice is becoming increasingly louder as he vents his frustration.

"She is my plaything." Fran's haughty voice stuns Clarke, and she begins to shake.

"That's enough. I've had enough. I am no one's plaything." Seeing the doubt in her parents' eyes and the smirk on Fran's face, Clarke rises. "Stop baiting them, Fran." Fran merely lifts an eyebrow. She can't take it anymore. "I'm leaving."

"Sit down, Clarke. Stop making a scene." Fran's voice is so condescending that Clarke sways on her feet. She's not sure whether she's going to pass out or throw up.

Clarke looks at Fran and it's as if she's never seen her before. Or it's possible she just hasn't been seeing her clearly for the last eight months. This is the Fran she used to know. The one she feared and admired, loved and hated. Maybe she is young and foolish. With tonight's display, Clarke wonders about Fran's feelings, about whether her parents are right that this is just some type of game for Fran. Shaking her head as tears fill her eyes, Clarke picks up her purse. "You three are supposed to be the ones who love me the most. If this is how you show your love, I don't want it."

She doesn't remember how she gets home. It's a blur of tears and despair. Letting herself into her apartment, she stumbles into her bedroom. How did such a wonderful day end so horribly? She doesn't know whether she has broken up with Fran, but at the very least it feels as if her rose-colored glasses have shattered. Clarke had forgotten how calculating Fran can be. And how callous. It was one of the reasons she left Haboob Software in the first place. The thought of enduring such condescension while dealing with her unrequited feelings sent her running. It seems that over time the memories of Fran's caustic behavior faded. How could she forget?

She leaves the lights off, not wanting to see the small gifts she has received from Fran. She placed them on a shelf near the window, little reminders that Fran was thinking of her, paying attention to what makes Clarke smile. Nor does she want to notice Fran's shirt hanging off her chair or her book on the side table. They stare at her like souvenirs.

Shucking off her dress, Clarke curls into a ball in the middle of her bed and begins to cry in earnest. *Happy birthday to me.* Bereft, Clarke's mind keeps rerunning the night's events like a silent horror movie. Sniffling, she finally falls into a restless sleep.

Chapter Seventeen

THE DEVIL'S DEAL

WATCHING THE LOVE OF her life walk away from her, Fran feels her control slip. *Not again. I can't lose her.* It nearly broke her last time, and that was before she knew how it feels to touch her, to be touched by her. A frisson of dread stabs Fran's heart—pinpricks of foreboding that Clarke's affections are turning into something else, thanks to her horrendous behavior.

"You don't deserve her," John says. Fran looks at John's irate features. His face is tight, eyes narrowed, and face red. He's angry, but no more than Fran is at herself for letting tonight devolve into a pissing contest. She's torn between running after Clarke and trying to make amends with her parents.

"True. However, surely you cannot expect me to turn her away. No, no, that is not a question. I let her walk away once. I do not have the strength to do so again. Therefore, I will remain with her for as long as she will have me." She sighs, her shoulders slumping. Although she sounds confident, she fears she's already lost Clarke. She has treated Clarke's parents as she treats those sycophants who mill around her, hoping to gain her favor with their corrosive tongues and seductive charm. They did not deserve such treatment. They are not interested in her power. Their sole concern is their daughter, and with the way she's behaved tonight, she cannot blame them.

"I just don't understand. You treated her horribly when she was your intern, yet she doesn't seem to care." Maureen shakes her head, eyes wide. She is a lovely woman with proud features and silver tresses threaded through her hair. She's wearing a conservative navy dress and silver drop earrings. Emotion dulls her dark eyes.

"It was a job. I expected her to complete her assignments in a quick and professional manner. She understands why I treated her that way. I simply cannot accept shoddy work. Regardless, she worked for me nearly seven years ago. She let it go. I suggest you do, too." Fran trains her eyes on her glass as she swirls the remaining wine. She wonders why she behaved like such a callous bitch.

"We may not be able to protect her from you, but we'll still see her on the holidays and her birthdays to talk some sense into her," John says. He's tall and broad-shouldered, dressed in black slacks, a maroon shirt opened at the throat, and a tan sports jacket. His jaw is smooth of stubble and hair slicked back. This is a man who cares about what others think and will do whatever he must to keep his daughter safe. Fran wants to do what's best for Clarke, too. She's realizing she needs to change her methods. First, though, she needs to come to an understanding about the holidays with her parents.

"Not quite. If you recall, she ceased communicating with you when you dismissed her feelings and attempted to brainwash her with your own. She is an adult, and she has the right to make her own decisions, even if you disapprove." She looks at their grim countenances and acknowledges, if only to herself, that she reinforced their concerns with tonight's show. It will take time to undo the damage. Speaking courteously to them now is a small first step, but it's one, nonetheless. "As for holidays and such, we will have to share such visits. I propose she travel to you for Thanksgiving and Easter. She shall remain here for Christmas, New Year's, and her birthday."

"Now wait a minute, Fran." Maureen's objection is expected.

"You are free to come here during those special occasions." Fran stares at them, waiting for their next objection. She's confident they won't extend the same courtesy of inviting her to their home. The resounding silence confirms her belief.

"Shouldn't this be Clarke's decision? I'm sure she'll want to spend the holidays with us and her childhood friends. Her other relatives, too." Maureen has a point, but Fran has learned over the years to appear unmoved when negotiating. This is the most important negotiation she's ever participated in. It will affect the rest of her life.

"Perhaps, but Clarke will feel better knowing we have discussed this ahead of time. Of course, we can make exceptions. The trading of holidays to deal with conflicting schedules and travel arrangements. Having a working framework will make future holidays easier on everyone." Fran reaches for her wine glass and reminds herself not to gulp down the remainder of the liquid. The more time she spends in the restaurant, the more time Clarke is alone, rethinking their relationship.

"I can't believe we're striking a deal with the devil," John says, guzzling the rest of his expensive whiskey as if it were cheap swill. Fran cheers internally. He's capitulating.

"You are welcome to join Clarke to visit us, as is your daughter. Clarke mentioned she's attending Columbia."

Surprised by Maureen's words, Fran nods. "She is. They get along well. In fact, Elaine is quite fond of Clarke. They often spend time together when I'm not available." She gazes at them for a moment and nods. "Thank you."

"Well, it's not like we have much choice." Fran ignores John's grumbling. It nearly makes Fran smile.

"John, please." Maureen places a hand on his arm, the exasperation in her voice clear.

Pressing her lips together, Fran tries once more to smooth everyone's ruffled feathers while making clear her feelings. She likes Clarke's parents. They don't pollute the air with ingratiating compliments and other fetid drivel. They are fighting for Clarke's happiness, as is Fran. They have a common goal, even if Clarke's parents don't quite realize it, yet.

"I won't let her go. The only reason we are having a conversation is because she will be extremely upset if you become estranged again. For Clarke's sake, I apologize for my part in upsetting you and your daughter." She raises a hand to get the server's attention to request the check and to have Clarke's half-eaten dinner placed in a to-go container.

"We probably could have handled this better. I regret what I said," John says.

"He's right. We could have behaved in a more civil manner," Maureen says. Fran can see where Clarke gets her manners. Even after becoming angry with her—rightfully so—they're quick to revert to a politeness many people do not use.

"Well. We're in agreement then. And the holiday schedule?" She signs her name on the bill and stands, Clarke's food in hand.

"Fine."

"Fine."

"Splendid. May I drop you off somewhere?"

"No. We're not far from here. We'll walk." John looks like he's run the gauntlet. She would feel bad if the stakes weren't so high.

"Have a pleasant evening. I'm sure Clarke will be in touch with you tomorrow." With a nod, Fran strides out of the restaurant. Her driver is waiting for her, and he is quick to open the passenger door. Fran isn't surprised Clarke didn't take the car to drop her off. Nor does she believe Clarke will be waiting for her in her home. She directs her driver to bring her to Clarke's apartment. She will not leave this until tomorrow. She will do what she must to correct her abysmal behavior.

Using her key, she enters the quiet apartment, walking through the darkened rooms with trepidation. She stalls in the bedroom doorway, her heart falling to her toes. She sees Clarke curled up in a ball on top of the bed in the lingerie Fran gifted her this morning. The moonlight shines through the open curtains, emphasizing the still-wet tears on her flushed cheeks.

Carding her fingers through Clarke's curly brown locks, Fran wonders how she can atone for her poor behavior. Reverting to her professional persona, a façade which has served her well over the years when dealing with threats, was instinctual. It was also the worst way to behave while meeting Clarke's parents for the first time. She behaved exactly the way her parents feared she would act, and in the process, she'd convinced them she was an unfeeling, manipulative, power-hungry bitch.

Watching Clarke's eyes blink open, one of her favorite moments when Clarke stays overnight, she murmurs her name, regret and sorrow dripping over the revered syllable. Clarke's stare sharpens as the previous events come to mind, and her face transforms into a scowl.

"Why are you here?" Clarke sits up. She swipes at her tears with angry motions.

"After you left, your parents and I had a nice chat." Fran tilts her head, purses her lips, and looks away. "They were upset with the way you departed and my role in it." Fran sighs, feeling older than dirt. Opening her heart has made her vulnerable, and her fallback actions have jeopardized her relationship with this magnificent creature. It is unacceptable. "I apologized for my behavior. You were right. I was provoking them."

Clarke gasps. Fran can see the whites of her eyes, stark against the shadows of her face. Her mouth drops open, but no words come out. Normally, Fran would find humor in Clarke's inability to speak, but for now she takes the opportunity to relate what happened after Clarke left.

"We have come to a type of understanding, an agreement, if you will. We have agreed that you will visit them for Thanksgiving and Easter, but that you will remain here for Christmas, New Year's Eve, and your birthday. They are welcome to visit during those times, and they have graciously invited me and Elaine on your excursions back to Massachusetts."

"Wait. You worked out a holiday visitation schedule?"

Clarke's confusion is endearing. And entirely justified. Fran admits, if only to herself, how odd this situation is. "I suppose that is an apt description."

"Don't I have a say in this? I'm not a little girl to be fought over in a custody battle, Fran."

"No, no. You are certainly not that." Fran moves closer to Clarke, taking her hand and holding on for dear life. "I became caught up in proving to your parents that you are mine, that they have no bearing on your feelings toward me." She brushes her thumb lightly over the top of Clarke's hand, relishing the softness. "When I watched you walk away from me, I realized how tenuous this relationship truly is and how few assurances you have provided." Fran's mouth tightens into a straight line. She knows Clarke loves her, but she doesn't actively participate in their relationship. Fran wonders at times why Clarke is so passive.

"Me? I—how can you doubt my feelings?"

"You don't talk to me when you are unhappy or upset. I am constantly having to guess what is occurring in that little head of yours." Fran sighs. "It's true you've gotten better, but you need to be a part of this relationship, Clarke. I need you to act like my equal. You need to believe you are."

Clarke stares at Fran, a furrow appearing on the bridge of her nose. She pulls her hand away, fisting the sheet next to her thigh. "Let me get this straight. You're saying you acted that way because I'm not acting the way you want me to?"

Shaking her head, Fran inhales through her nose, determined to resolve this nonsense and get on with the birthday celebration. "No, that is not what I am saying. Tonight devolved into that powerplay due to my insecurities. I'm explaining my motivation, the reason why I acted the way I did. I didn't realize until tonight that I need you to communicate more with me. I know I'm not the best at discussing my feelings, and maybe this is the pot calling the kettle black, but I need you to tell me what you're feeling. Especially when you're upset or worried or angry."

"I'm sorry, Fran. I just always figured that you knew—that you know—how much I love you, how much I need you. The rest—" Clarke waves a hand in the air before placing it on Fran's. "It's much more important to me that you're happy. I don't ever want to do anything to jeopardize that." Clarke looks down at the bedspread.

"What makes me happy is knowing what you're thinking. Being able to believe that when I make a suggestion, you agree to it because you want to do it and not because you think it will make me happy. Having you be an active participant when making plans. Leveling up. You are my equal in every way, Clarke. It's time for you to believe it."

"I don't want you to doubt me, to doubt us. I want you to trust me. I'll do better."

"Me, too. I treated you like a possession tonight." Fran lifts Clarke's hand and kisses the back of it. "For that I am sorry. You deserve better."

"Wait, how did you get my parents to calm down?"

Fran smiles mysteriously. "That is a story for another time." She pulls out a jewelry box from her purse and presents it to Clarke. "I planned on giving this to you earlier. Happy birthday." She watches as Clarke opens it.

"Oh my god." Clarke's whispered words hang in the air. She lifts out the gift, a diamond tennis bracelet. Even in the dark, it seems to glow. "It's beautiful. You didn't have to. You've already given me so much. All I need is you."

"Oh, let an old woman spend her money as she wishes." Fran smirks at the old person joke and Clarke's typical squawk of outrage. She takes the bracelet out of Clarke's hands. "May I?" At her nod Fran secures the clasp on her. Lifting Clarke's forearm, she kisses the inside of her wrist. "Beautiful."

"Thank you, Fran. I love it." Clarke leans in to kiss her. "I love you." Clarke's wide smile reassures Fran that they will recover from the disastrous evening, but she's not ready to move on.

Fran runs the back of her fingers over one of Clarke's cheeks. "Were you crying?"

"I thought I'd lost you." Clarke looks away, her eyes beginning to shine.

Fran regrets bringing it up. The last thing she wants is for Clarke to become upset again, but if they don't address this now, it may come up again during a disagreement. It's better to work through these feelings now. She's always been good at looking ahead, and Fran plans on having Clarke next to her each and every day.

"I was afraid that you didn't really care for me." Clarke's meek words, imbued with so much sorrow, make Fran's eyes water.

Blinking away her tears, Fran uses gentle fingers to lift Clarke's chin so she can gaze at her. "That couldn't be further from the truth. I've tried so hard to show you how I truly feel, but sometimes when I feel threatened, I resort to acting as I do at Haboob. I feel more in my element. It is clear your parents love you. I was afraid they would convince you that I am not good enough for you because the truth is, I'm not."

"That's not true. They couldn't do that."

"Couldn't they?" Fran grimaces, sadness washing through her. "They'd be right. I proved that tonight."

"Why is it so hard for you to believe that I love you?"

Clarke's passionate question startles Fran. It also gives her hope. She wants to release these insecurities and believe whole-heartedly that Clarke knows what she wants. Who she wants. Dare she believe Clarke genuinely wants her?

"Fran, I know how I feel. I may seem naïve or inexperienced, but it's not true. Jesus! What do I have to do?" Clarke looks out her window, her chin tilted up in defiance, her chest heaving.

"Move in with me."

"What?" Clarke peers into Fran's eyes, a wondrous look on her face. "Did you say move in with you?" Fran merely nods. "Are you sure? You're not just saying that because of what happened tonight are you? We don't have to—"

"Clarke Parson, do you or do you not want to live with me?"

"I do! I just, why would you want to live with me?"

Fran feels elation fill her, and she lets loose a loud laugh, pulling Clarke into a fierce hug. "You silly, silly girl! Why?" Fran pulls back to stare at her. "Because I love you, and I need you with me every day." She leans in to capture Clarke's pouty lips, feeling ravenous on so many levels. She enters Clarke's mouth, devouring her whimpers and rubbing their tongues together for a delicious, thorough reacquaintance before releasing her. She leans back to peer into hooded eyes. "Well?"

"Yes. Yes, I want to be with you. I'll give my property manager notice tomorrow."

"Good. Come home with me, Clarke." She stares at Clarke, willing her to agree.

"Okay."

They grin at one another like idiots, but Fran doesn't care a bit. Tomorrow they can talk more. Tomorrow they will enter the next phase in their lives. It will be glorious. And lovely. And perfect. Fran is certain. And regardless of what the future brings, Fran is convinced that they will face it together, and their commitment to one another will only deepen. Clarke may have walked away again, but this time Fran went after her. And she convinced her to come back.

Chapter Eighteen

LEVELING UP

WALKING THROUGH HER EMPTY apartment, Clarke takes time to make sure she hasn't left anything behind. She has stacked her packed boxes in neat rows near the apartment door. She shakes her head at the small amount—a dozen boxes and two pieces of luggage contain her entire life while living in New York. She donated her furniture, knowing she won't need any of the pieces, as well as clothes she hasn't worn in years. Besides the clothes she's kept, what's left are books, knick-knacks, and framed photos.

In some ways, she's sad to be moving. She learned some harsh lessons while living alone for the first time. She learned how to navigate school, work, and love. She learned how to set a budget and stick to it. She learned that she can't trust everyone, but she can trust some. She learned the difference between an acquaintance and a friend. And she learned what true love feels like.

Hoping to get her security deposit and last month's rent back, Clarke has scrubbed every inch of the place. This is the one time she's glad it's so small. Half of her clothes are already in Fran's home. Really what she's packed in the luggage are the bulky winter clothes it's not yet cold enough to wear. She's looking forward to winter. Her apartment didn't afford her any good views, but Fran's co-op overlooks the Hudson River on one side and a quiet tree-lined street on the other side. Since she often works from home, she's excited to watch snow fall once wintery weather blows in. She's excited to sit in front of a roaring fire under decadent, soft blankets. She's excited to watch the world turn into a white wonderland.

The process of moving in with Fran has been harder than she first anticipated. Fran and Clarke had to complete a request form to add a household member to Fran's co-op. She feared Fran would rescind her offer once she saw Clarke's financials, but she laughed at Clarke's fears.

"You do realize you're a rising star, don't you? You have a steady income, to the extent that you're adding to your savings account every month. Besides, do you really believe I asked you to move in with me to help with expenses?" Fran looked at her as if she was the most precious thing she'd ever seen.

"But I do want to help with the expenses. It's only fair." Clarke doesn't want to live off Fran's wealth, not for necessities. She'd rather they split the monthly expenses.

"If it's that important to you, we can sit down and sort it out." And they did. Clarke feels more like Fran's partner in every way. Over time, Clarke is planning to purchase furniture and help turn Fran's apartment into their home. That reminds her of a videogame idea she has for players to design rooms to fit two distinct personalities. She pulls out her phone to capture some thoughts on it, only stopping when the movers arrive. She hitches a ride with them, and two hours later, she's alone in her new home.

She remembers the last time she was here without Fran. By then they had keys to each other's homes, and Fran was working long hours. On that occasion, Fran had to travel to Philadelphia and wasn't set to return until the next day. Missing her, Clarke had decided to work and sleep in Fran's apartment, hoping it would dull the sharp sting of missing her. She set up her laptop in Fran's den, wanting to be surrounded by Fran's energy, permeated by her ambiance, reminded of her essence.

Clarke couldn't help feeling cold and bereft, constantly hungry and dissatisfied. She took to sitting in Fran's study, reviewing the mocked-up video game Fran designed for her, the one that brought them back together. It wasn't enough. At the end of the day, Clarke was alone. She received no kisses or tight embraces. She was unable to stare at Fran until her eyes drooped or run her fingers over well-known back muscles. She wandered around, lost. Shaking herself out of that memory, Clarke reminds herself that Fran is in town, at work, and they will be together soon.

Although tempted to unpack without delay, she wants to discuss with Fran where to place her belongings. Hearing her cell phone ring, she glances at the face and smiles. *Speak of the devil.*

"Hi. I was just thinking of you." Clarke takes a seat on the small loveseat in the den, closing her eyes as she listens to Fran's voice.

"I like that. Where are you?" Fran's husky voice is music to Clarke's ears.

"At home. Our home. I was thinking that we didn't really discuss where I should place my belongings."

"Well, if you're not in a hurry, we can figure that out tonight. For now, I cleared half of the closet and one of the dressers for your clothes. I also made room on the bookshelves for you."

Clarke climbs the stairs and enters their bedroom, peeking in the closet to see how much space is available. *More than enough space.* She smiles when she notices some of her clothes are already on hangers. "Thanks. It looks like there's enough space for my clothes."

"Good. I've been thinking about you all morning. You're terribly distracting. Harry's accused me of ignoring him several times during our meeting today, which may be true. Are you working later?"

"No. I have a lull between projects. It's perfect. This way I can get settled." Clarke tries to sound upbeat. In truth, she always becomes nervous when she doesn't have a project to work on. She falls into her old insecurities that she isn't good enough, that no one believes she's talented.

"How do you feel about coming to Haboob to help one of the graphic designers? She's having trouble with a character's movements, and we have a short deadline."

"Wouldn't that be considered nepotism?" Clarke is only half-kidding. Their romance is still private enough that most people don't know, but she would hate for anyone to look at her as if she's taking advantage of it to get ahead in her career.

"Darling, everyone knows you're talented. Your name is everywhere, and you've won awards for your work. I'll sweeten the deal by taking you to dinner later—your choice. Please?"

"Okay. Give me an hour. Thanks for the job, boss."

"If you'd rather not..."

"No, no. I want to do it. Really." Clarke feels bad for teasing Fran. She's been nothing but supportive, and Clarke knows how hard she's worked to help Clarke feel like an equal. "I don't have any deadlines right now, and you know how I get when I have nothing to do. I'll see you soon."

Once they disconnect the call, Clarke retrieves the two pieces of luggage to unpack her clothes. When she opens the dresser, she sees Fran has placed the clothes she left from previous visits in the top two drawers. She feels her heart flutter. It's these small actions that reaffirm how considerate Fran can be.

It doesn't take her long to unpack. She takes a quick shower and runs out of the apartment to catch the B line to Rockefeller Center, but finds Fran's driver leaning against the town car, waiting for her. He straightens up when he sees her, dipping his head in greeting.

"Fran sent me. Hop in."

Although she feels weird sitting in the back without Fran, she slides onto the leather seat without comment. They arrive much sooner than she would have by subway, and Clarke makes her way inside with a pep in her step.

Knocking on the doorjamb to Fran's office, Clarke offers a smile to her and to Harry, who is pointing at something on the laptop in front of them.

"Hello, Cap. Fran told me you were coming to rescue our beleaguered design team. Fitz is waiting for you."

"Right. Let me get to it, then." She offers a small wave before scampering to the main bullpen. She recognizes some of the employees from the *End of the World, the Greenhouse Effect* project, and they exchange greetings as she continues to Jan Fitzgerald's side. Fitz is a quirky redhead who can run rings around her, so she's curious to see what's slowing her down.

"Hey, Fitz. How're you doing?" Clarke plops down on a chair next to her.

"Oh, hi. I'm doing great." She peers at Clarke, and her eyebrows shoot up. "Wait! You're the ringer, aren't you? Thank God the calvary is here. I bet you can help me on this. I've been wracking my brain." She turns back to her computer, fingers flying over the keyboard. She pulls up a split screen with one side reflecting a character and the other side an actor. She runs both simultaneously, and Clarke leans forward, squinting her eyes. Instead of matching the actor's movements, the animation is jerky, making it clear where each movement begins and ends. The twenty-second comparison ends, and Jan swivels her head, a look of expectation on her face.

"Right. I can see the problem. Which programs are you using?"

"Motion Matching for Unity and Blender."

"I attended a conference in April where they were talking about using Motion Matching with Unreal Engine. It smooths out the transitions. Do you have Unreal Engine?"

"Yeah, but I'm not well-versed in them." Jan is quick to pull up the software and load the motion capture files.

"I'll show you some tricks I learned. It will cut down the production time for you." Clarke moves closer and takes a few minutes to click through the video. "Okay, so here, you do this." She clicks over to the correct tool and shows Jan. After about ten minutes she can see Jan's getting the hang of it. Sitting back, she watches as the video character moves across the screen. "That looks much better."

"Yeah, it does. Thanks, Clarke. Can you walk me through more of the program's protocols, so I'll be able to use it on my own? You're saving my butt."

"Sure. The entire point of my being here is to help you with the new processes. It's no problem to show you. I'm glad to share the information." She hears a voice clearing and looks up to see Harry standing behind them, a smirk on his face.

"Actually, if you don't mind, Cap, I'd like to call the team together so all of them can learn the processes. We can set up in the conference room."

Surprised, Clarke nods her head. She didn't realize she'd be teaching a master class, but she doesn't mind helping. She opens her phone to shoot a text to Fran. "Looks like I'm going to be hard at work for a while. I look forward to a fabulous dinner at Café Pierre."

A moment later, she receives a response. "Your wish is my command."

Feeling as if warm molasses is being poured over her soul, Clarke bites back a smile. She's starting to believe Fran is telling the truth, that she'll do anything to make Clarke happy. Her actions have proven her sincerity repeatedly.

Two hours later, Clarke has finished presenting the basics for the processes and walked the team through all the tips and tricks she knows. They've worked on small portions of five characters for the game they're developing, something to do with deep-sea adventures. The added trickiness of creating facial expressions while the characters are underwater is a fun challenge.

Once they finish the impromptu training, Harry asks Clarke to remain in the room as the others file out. "Thanks for coming to our rescue. I have a proposal for you, and before you ask, I've already passed this by Fran. Whatever your answer, you can be sure that we'll still be calling on you to work on different projects with us in the future. We value your expertise, your creativeness, and your loyalty."

"Thanks. That's nice of you to say. What's the proposal?" Clarke feels anticipation buzz through her. She has no idea what Harry is leading up to, but even the promise of future collaborations is thrilling.

"I'm being promoted to creative director, and I want you to consider becoming the old me. You just showed everyone that you'll be a great lead designer. You know the latest software, you work well with the team, and you're good under pressure." He leans against the table, arms loosely folded against his chest. "So, what do you think?"

"Wait. Was this whole thing a setup to make sure I can do it?" Her brain's snapping so many synapses she's afraid it will short-circuit. She's not sure how she feels about the subterfuge.

"Not in the sense that we thought you couldn't do it. Even if we hadn't had you come in today to help the team, we would have offered you the job. Today's demonstration was serendipitous. It showed the team and you that you'll be a great lead. So, what do you say? Want to become my number one?"

"Will I be able to work on side projects as long as they're not video games from the competition?"

"Such as?"

"Movies, television, maybe book adaptions." She shrugs.

"You drive a hard bargain." Harry hands her a document, and after skimming through it, she chuckles.

It includes a clause stating she can work on other multimedia projects outside of Haboob as long as no conflict of interest is present, and she doesn't share any intellectual property without written authorization. "What about my relationship with Fran?"

"I already notified HR. They'll want you to sign some paperwork." Turning to the door, Clarke smiles at Fran as she walks toward them. "Any other questions?"

"Do you have a pen?"

"I do." She hands Clarke a black case, and Clarke opens it to find a gold-plated Mont Blanc pen with a ruby gemstone on the cap's clip. Clarke gasps. She's never seen such a beautiful pen. She takes it out of the case, admiring the workmanship. Glancing at Fran, she sees affection in her smile and a proud gleam in her eyes. As soon as Clarke signs the employment agreement, she hears a pop.

Jumping at the unexpected sound, she joins in with the chuckles from team members who've rejoined them, champagne in hand.

"Pretty sure of yourself, weren't you?" Clarke says in a soft voice to Fran. "How did you know I'd agree?"

"I didn't. I just hoped for the best and planned for it." Her lips curl into a small smile. "You know I'm a woman of action." Clarke can't argue with that.

The team gathers around Clarke, welcoming her into the fold. Since she knows most of them, it feels like a homecoming. For the first time in her life, she feels like she's where she's meant to be, doing what she's meant to be doing, while standing next to the person with whom she's meant to share her life. Fran's hand on her lower back keeps her grounded. She half-believes she would float to the ceiling if Fran weren't here to tether her.

Once the small gathering breaks up, Fran excuses herself to gather her belongings from her office before they leave for dinner. Harry gathers the used glasses and takes them to the break room. Clarke sits on the edge of the conference table, thinking about all the items she needs to complete before she transitions to this new job.

As if reading her mind, Harry says, "I don't know whether you saw the start date, but we dated it for a week from now so you can wrap up any projects you're working on. Will that be enough time?" Harry pours the rest of the champagne into her plastic cup as he speaks.

"Yes. That's perfect. Thank you. It will be fun to work with you again."

"I'm looking forward to it." Harry taps his cup to hers and says, "Cheers." He turns toward the door when Fran reenters. "Now, finish that and get out of here before you get sucked into more work."

"Technically, she doesn't start until next week, so your threat has no merit, which you know since you pointed it out to her mere moments ago." Fran's voice carries a hint of humor.

"The boss hears everything." He winks at Clarke and turns to Fran. "Aye-aye, *mon capitaine*." He salutes Fran and walks to the door. "Have a great night, ladies."

Clarke chuckles at the second reference to Star Trek. She has no doubt they'll succeed in having a fantastic night. The expression on Fran's face promises she'll make it so.

Chapter Nineteen

FINDING RELIEF

RAIN HITS THE WINDOWPANES, disturbing Fran's restless sleep. Another night without Clarke by her side. Sighing, Fran rolls over to stare at the San Franciscan weather balefully. Clarke has ruined her. For two months they've lived together, and Fran has found herself unable to concentrate on her work during this week's separation. She huffs in exasperation. What a waste of time. All week she has attended countless panels, luncheons, and soirées. And for the first time since she became the CEO of Haboob Software, she does not want to be here. She misses Clarke. It is unbearable.

The first annual gaming conference she attended after Clarke left her employ, Fran worked hard not to think about her. It was during that same annual conference, the one they attended together, when Fran's feelings crystallized. She watched Clarke enter the hall while laughing with another intern, and a swooping feeling nearly dropped Fran to the ground. The realization that she'd fallen for an intern was jarring, horrifying, untenable. She couldn't act on her feelings. Not while Clarke was beginning her career. Not while Fran was solidifying her own professional standing. No, the timing was wrong. She couldn't offer anything to Clarke. She had to let her go.

With that in mind, she'd sent Clarke on her way with a glowing recommendation and a heartfelt wish that she be happy. After she left, Fran strictly kept her mind focused on the company. And as the years passed, the ache dulled. However, now that she has Clarke in her life, in her heart, now that she is living with the woman and discovering more reasons to love her every day, Fran feels bereft not falling asleep or waking up next to the younger woman. Each day away makes Fran feel more restless, and she is about ready to climb out of her skin. She wants Clarke next to her today, now, and every day thereafter.

With their schedules, it is common for one of them to already be in bed when the other arrives home. It doesn't matter. They're able to share passionate kisses late at night and awaken to loving hugs each morning. That's what she misses the most—the connection. Now that she knows how it feels to share her life with such an incredible person, she loathes being without Clarke.

Noticing the time, Fran groans, placing the back of her hand over her eyes like some damsel in distress. Inhaling deeply, she sits up with a sigh. Two more days. Two more days of being the Queen of Games before she can return to New York and hold Clarke in her arms. In some ways, knowing this makes her feel more desperate. It's like running a marathon and seeing the finish line up ahead. She can feel her body starting to fall apart, and she doesn't know how to hold it together so she can cross the finish line.

Every night she has spoken with Clarke for a few, precious moments. Each day she receives short texts. It is not enough. When Fran falls into a restless sleep each night, she hugs the pillow, yearning for it to be Clarke in her arms. She doesn't know how she'll survive another day without her. She doesn't know how she became so needy. So pathetic. Nevertheless, Fran cannot deny how empty she feels not being able to touch Clarke. One thing she does know is that she will not allow them to remain apart for so long again. She just needs to get through today and tomorrow.

Hearing a knock, Fran rises, wrapping her robe around her tightly and doing her best to tamp down her messy hair and sour mood before opening the door. Harry stands there, several pieces of paper in his hand. He smiles as Fran opens the door wide enough for him to enter.

"Good morning, mon capitaine," he says in much too good a mood as he brushes past her. He walks straight to the telephone, picks it up, and orders room service for two.

"Did we schedule a breakfast meeting that I'm unaware of?" Fran asks sardonically.

"No, but we are both in desperate need of caffeine, and we both know that if we don't eat now, we won't eat all day."

"Hmmm." Fran realizes he's right as she wearily sinks into a high-back, winged chair. Crossing her legs, she takes the proffered documents and dons her glasses to review them. They begin comparing notes from the day before, and Fran becomes more short-tempered with each moment that passes.

She loves her work. Truly she does. But she loves Clarke more, and that realization scares her immensely. *Does she even miss me?*

"All right, Fran. I didn't want to have to do this, but clearly, I have no choice," Harry says grimly.

"Whatever are you going on about?" Fran asks as she pins him with her signature glare, aggravated by the tone of his voice and the determination in his eyes. She does not have time for such nonsense.

"You are going home. Today."

"Don't be absurd. We have two more days of panels, meetings, and schmoozing. I cannot possibly leave early." Although Fran dismisses the idea out of hand, she wishes she could do as he's suggesting.

"No, no," Harry says, waving his finger in front of her face. "We can have you on a plane by noon. You'll only miss the afternoon panels today and tonight's wrap-up, but I will stand in for you." He gazes at her pensively. "You really miss her, don't you?"

Fran opens her mouth to refute his statement, but she cannot bring herself to lie. She does miss Clarke. Desperately. She can feel herself flushing as she delivers a slight nod, more of a tilt of the head than anything else. She can feel emotions building behind her eyes, and the gut-wrenching feeling of discontent gnaws at her incessantly. She blinks several times as she glances away from Harry's knowing look, needing a moment to control her chaotic emotions. She wants to go home. Of course she does, but she has a job to do, too. Can she justify leaving early? Will anyone care? Will it make Clarke happy?

A knock at the door signals their food has arrived. They eat in companionable silence, Fran wondering whether Clarke has been taking care of herself while they have been apart. She does love watching Clarke eat. Her lover has such a healthy appetite.

Taking out her cell phone, Fran quickly types, *Thinking of you, darling. I can't wait to hold you in my arms again. F xoxo*

"Tell her I said hello," Harry says with a cheeky smile.

Fran tags on Harry's greeting before sending the text. "Arrange for me to fly out after the leadership roundtable," Fran says softly before taking one more sip of her coffee and rising. "I am going to get ready." She stops at her bedroom door and turns to Harry once more. "And Harry," she says, capturing his eyes and smiling slightly. "Thank you."

Feeling her phone vibrate as she closes the bedroom door, Fran feels her spirits rise as she reads Clarke's response. This woman has turned her upside down. What surprises her is how she likes viewing her world from this new vantage point.

I miss you so much. You'd better rest up, lady. I intend to make up for lost time once you come home. Love you. C

This is the right decision. She is ready to get back to the person who holds her heart. With a spring in her step, Fran refocuses on what must happen before she can find her way back to Clarke.

The return flight provides Fran with an opportunity to rest. She does not want to be too tired when she arrives home since she has every intention of reacquainting herself with every inch of Clarke's delectable body. She indulges in thoughts of how she will touch her lover, how she will evoke those breathless moans and pleading mewls. God, she has missed her.

Feeling the week's whirlwind schedule catching up with her, Fran calls over a flight attendant and directs her to awaken her an hour before they land. Only after the flight attendant reassures her that she will do as Fran has asked does she allow herself to close her eyes. Her final thoughts are of Clarke's wide smile and beaming chocolate eyes, lightening up to a golden hue when she's happy. Soon she will see them in person.

As soon as Fran walks through her front door, she feels the stress of their separation ease. No lights are on downstairs, but she is sure Clarke is home. She waves toward the corner, and her driver deposits her luggage in the front parlor before leaving. She removes her coat quickly and climbs the stairs to their bedroom, eager to see Clarke.

Halfway to her destination, she pauses. She could swear she hears Clarke moaning her name. Reaching the open bedroom door, Fran covers her mouth with her hand as she watches Clarke trying desperately to reach completion by her own hand. The tableau is so erotic she feels her body heat up immediately and her nipples harden. Fran removes her clothes in a hurry, her eyes fastened on Clarke's body as she struggles to find relief. Fran's body clenches as she hears her name shouted, and the proof of Fran's arousal from watching Clarke coats her inner thighs.

Not able to stay away any longer, Fran crosses the room swiftly and captures parted lips as her fingers seek out Clarke's swollen clit. She doesn't allow Clarke to remove the two fingers she has buried inside herself. Instead, she cups the hand as they kiss and kiss and kiss. It is divine.

Ravenously, Fran sucks on a forceful tongue, tasting desperation, and relief, and desire. Finally releasing now-swollen lips, Fran mouths Clarke's breast, sucking on the nipple as she presses against Clarke's hand, creating a rhythm while rocking against her. She loves the sounds coming out of Clarke, the grunts and whines as her body responds to Fran.

Words pour out of Fran, stored up during their days of separation. "You're amazing. I missed you so much. I was such a mess that I couldn't stay away any longer. I took an earlier flight home immediately after the leadership roundtable." She whispers how much she has missed Clarke, how wonderful she is, how she had to return home early to be with her. Fran switches breasts, nibbling on the tight nub. "I dreamt of you. Fantasized about how I would touch you once I returned."

The fantasies she indulged in late at night over the past week are pale in comparison to the reality of this luscious body undulating under her. She feels so hungry, and only loving Clarke can slake such a relentless thirst. The yearning to be closer to this woman has consumed her thoughts and having her in her arms again is nearly enough to remove all her self-control.

As she shimmies down to lick the sensitive nerve center currently standing at attention, Fran grins savagely. Clarke is hers. She was fantasizing about Fran as she sought release moments ago. Knowing that Clarke is true to her even within the privacy of her carnal thoughts rockets Fran's confidence into the stratosphere. It reassures her in a profound way that Clarke loves her unconditionally, absolutely, unequivocally.

Clarke's body speeds up as Fran pours out her heart, her dreams, her need to be with Clarke. Fran finds it easy to express herself through this steady stream of words. Every word she speaks is the truth. She pushes her finger in between the two sliding in and out of Clarke's slick passage, wanting to feel Clarke's inner walls pulsating, wanting to be closer.

"I, oh my god." Clarke's words, imbued with such emotion, signal her imminent arrival at her peak. Fran's body is keeping pace, ready to explode with the mother of all orgasms, even without the direct stimulus of Clarke's touch.

"Fantasies can never come close to how you truly feel in my arms. I can't get enough of you. Can never get enough." Fran's voice is gruff, a consequence of the emotions that have overwhelmed her. She reveals her heart, no longer afraid of exposing herself in this way. She's learned that her heart is safe in Clarke's keeping.

Those words throw Clarke over the brink. Her legs shake and calves flex as Fran's world dims and all sensation focuses on tasting the proof of Clarke's desire, on feeling it through their commingled, thrusting fingers. Clarke's joyful shout compels her to look up, and she watches greedily as Clarke freezes in the air as ecstasy overtakes her. This is Fran's sustenance. Her body reacts to the gorgeous display of wanton uninhibitedness, and she rides out her resulting blissful orgasm. *God, I needed that!* she thinks in a daze as her body slows down.

Clarke has passed out. Of course. She usually does for a few minutes after she reaches completion. Smiling tenderly, Fran removes their hands from their snug haven and moves up to embrace Clarke. She runs her fingers through sweaty locks rhythmically, so damn glad she's home. She cannot imagine not having Clarke in her life. Not now. Not here. Their lives have become so intertwined, and she knows Clarke will not leave her again. She wants to show everyone this amazing woman, wants everyone to see how happy this woman makes her feel. It's time they make a statement to the world, to each other. It's time to claim Clarke publicly. And in return she will allow Clarke to claim her.

Before opening her eyes, Clarke breathes deeply and exhales. She wraps her arms around Fran and hugs her close, humming as Fran delivers butterfly kisses to her shoulder and neck. Looking down, she watches Clarke's eyelids flutter open. Her eyes glow with affection, tinged with awe, as if she can't believe Fran is with her. Her fingers explore the contours of Fran's face, and an infectious smile crosses Clarke's lovely visage.

"What are you smiling about?" Fran feels amusement steal through her. Interlacing their fingers Fran lifts their hands to her lips to kiss. She can tell Clarke is bursting with questions, but she is obviously exhausted. She has not taken care of herself during Fran's absence, so sleep is more essential than important questions.

"You're home." Clarke sighs happily.

Fran rakes her fingers through Clarke's mussed hair and hears her sigh again, as if she were some Victorian heroine whose lover has returned from the war. "Yes, I'm here."

"I missed you." Clarke is mumbling, a sure sign she'll fall asleep soon.

"I noticed." She ghosts her lips over Clarke's flushed cheek. "Sleep, Clarke. We can talk tomorrow."

Clarke doesn't need Fran to tell her twice. Before succumbing to sleep she says, "I love you."

"I know." Fran continues to slide her fingers through the appealing tousle of curls, leaning in to graze her lips against Clarke's forehead.

Her earlier fear that Clarke might not have missed her was obviously unfounded. She has witnessed all she needs to know, shining through luminescent eyes. Fran settles down next to her love, holding her close as Clarke falls into an exhausted sleep, and she smiles. Returning home early was the right decision. Clarke is her home.

The next morning, they lounge in bed well past sunrise. Clarke had taken the day off in anticipation of Fran's return, and Fran has a free day since she returned sooner than scheduled.

"Darling, I have a question to ask you. Will you accompany me to this year's Breast Cancer Awareness benefit next month?" Fran runs her fingers down Clarke's arm with soothing strokes.

"I'd love to."

Fran can see the concern in Clarke's eyes and appreciates how that doesn't stop her from agreeing to go. Even though the papers have continued to snap pictures of them when they dine in public, speculation has petered out with their lack of substantiation. Attending the benefit will change all that by sending a clear message that they are together.

"Are you sure?" Clarke asks.

Fran searches Clarke's eyes. "I want to. It's time. Clear?" Clarke nods, relief passing over her face. Fran's relieved, too. She wants to present a united front, a clear message that they're together. It wasn't that long ago when she thought she'd lost Clarke. It would have changed her world from the brilliant hues of color Clarke has gifted her to a world of gray. She'll do whatever she can to make sure that doesn't happen. Attending the benefit together will serve as a good start.

As their eyes meet once more, Fran's heart dances a little jig. She feels peace settle over her, knowing Clarke misses her when she's away, loves her with a passion that makes Fran breathless, and needs her near whenever possible. Finally, Fran knows that Clarke won't walk away from her again, not now that she's proven to Clarke that her heart is safe, that she'd rather rip out her own heart than hurt her. With this proof, Fran is certain nothing will stop her from being with this incredible woman for the rest of her life. Not the mistakes she's made, or the fear Clarke has felt, or people who seek to tear them apart. They are together, and they will walk down life's path hand in hand.

Chapter Twenty

TAKING DECISIVE ACTION

AS SHE GLIDES ACROSS the ballroom to rejoin Fran, Clarke pretends not to hear the whispers. Most comments are positive. She takes full responsibility for that. Each time someone has approached them tonight, Clarke has taken pains to engage the person in conversation. Most seem eager for the chance to bask in Fran's powerful aura, and Clarke sees no harm in representing herself in this way. She wants people to accept her, if only so Fran will not need to deal with any fallout.

Reaching Fran's side, Clarke offers a flute of champagne, momentarily dazzled by her smile of thanks. Fran seems at ease. Clarke is glad. Although Fran is not a keynote speaker, Brightman-Cook is a sponsor for this event, and many of the heavyweights are present. *The wealthy and influential mill around, eventually coming to pay their respects to the Queen of Games and her consort.* If her thoughts echo with a tinge of sarcasm, she doesn't let it show on her face. She keeps a placid smile directed toward each person who approaches them.

Clarke allows her gaze to wander until she feels an unpleasant change in the air. Fran straightens up, her eyes becoming sharper. Following Fran's stare, Clarke looks into the eyes of James Lowry, the creepiest guy she's ever met.

"Clarke Parson, a pleasure to see you again," James says as he kisses the back of her hand. Clarke just manages not to pull her hand away. "Fran." He nods in her direction before refocusing on Clarke. He takes his time to rake his eyes over her body from head to toe and back. Clarke feels revulsion rise thickly in her throat. She swallows it down. His beady eyes stare at her décolletage brazenly. Clarke feels Fran's rage and seeks to ward off the ensuing storm.

"Hello, Mr. Lowry. It's so nice to see you again. Is your wife joining you tonight?" Clarke asks the question using a syrupy voice, knowing it's better to play nice. She feels Fran's arm slip around her waist.

"Not tonight. She's a bit under the weather. You look ravishing, my dear. Simply ravishing." James takes the opportunity to stare at her body once more as Fran stiffens in outrage. She knows Fran won't allow much more of this. She needs to act as if he doesn't make her want to take a hot shower to wash off his filthy stench.

"Thank you. You can't go wrong in Versace." Clarke answers in a bright voice even though she wants to gag. Turning to Fran, Clarke continues. "Fran gave it to me as a gift. Her taste is impeccable."

"Mmm, I have to agree." James's leering is getting on Clarke's nerves. "Fran always did like the best. I suspect you must be exceptionally good." *Okay, so that's just rude.*

"James, we'd love to stay and chat, but we were just about to leave." Clarke must hand it to Fran for remaining so restrained. Personally, Clarke wants to rip the contemptible man to pieces.

"Leaving so soon? Well, I suppose that is why you are with such a young woman, so she can service your needs. Although, it is no longer a secret, Fran. The board will be concerned with how your indiscretions may affect Haboob Software's interests. Particularly after I get through with them." James has the nerve to lean in closer to say quietly, "But if you are willing to share..." He smirks at their shocked faces.

Clarke recovers first. Not caring to cover her anger, she steps into his space. "You must be highly delusional if you think that I would ever consent to such an arrangement. You are a sad, little man." Clarke feels her eyes spit fire at him, empowered when he steps back uncertainly. "You know, James—may I call you James? I came across some interesting information a few months ago that points toward some unorthodox actions by a certain CEO to seal the deal with his largest client. Nowadays, cameras are all over the place. It's not hard to track down recordings, and I'm sure you're aware that cell phone records can be resurrected, even after they're erased." Clarke glides a hand down a shaking arm as she watches his face pale. "Do you think the military would approve? If someone revealed those actions, well, I think they might want to reconsider their relationship with you."

Pretending not to notice Fran's riveted attention or James's increasing apprehension, Clarke continues. "Originally, I was thinking about contacting an investigative reporter at *The New York Times*, but I tossed the idea away since the blowback might hurt Brightman-Cook and indirectly Haboob Software. Now I'm beginning to think I might want to hand that information over to some interested individuals who work for the government. What do you think, James?" Clarke bats her eyelashes at him, relishing his expression when he realizes his impotence. She waits patiently for his response.

He steps away carefully and joins his hands together as if about to pray. Maybe he is. "I misjudged you. It seems you and Fran are well-suited after all." An interesting mixture of respect and dislike flash through his eyes. Clarke can live with that.

"Yes. We are." Turning to Fran, Clarke smiles coyly at her. "Shall we go?" With Fran's dazed consent, they sweep out of the room into the crisp evening air. Fran stays quiet the entire ride home but holds Clarke's hand in a tight clasp. Clarke wonders whether Fran is angry with her for threatening James. She knows that's usually Fran's role, one she enjoys.

Once home Clarke removes Fran's wrap from her shoulders and notices she is trembling. "Fran?"

Shaking her head in response, she leads the way up the stairs to the master suite without saying a word. Not able to bear the thought that Fran is angry with her, Clarke tries again.

"Are you—are you angry with me?" She shrinks back a little when Fran whips toward her.

"All these years I have battled with that vile, little man." Fran stalks toward Clarke, who backs up against the door. "All these years and no one has ever dared to threaten him on my behalf." Fran stands nose-to-nose with Clarke.

She's not sure what to think. Fran is obviously riled, but she doesn't exactly seem upset.

"Am I angry?" Fran chuckles. "Hardly. I have never been so aroused in my life." Fran yanks her head forward for a rough kiss.

Oh. Clarke feels ravenous hands sliding up the slit on her right thigh and the exposed area of her back. *She isn't angry at all.*

Clarke's hands scrabble over Fran's back, searching for the zipper to the gown. Fran is wearing a gorgeous long-sleeved, embroidered gown by Oscar de la Renta. The black semitransparent silk organza is hand-stitched with a complex design of sequins and pearls. Clarke must push down her desire to rip the dress off Fran. Not one to normally care about designer clothes, Fran made the exception for this event, knowing photographers would be taking pictures of them together. After tearing her lips away, Clarke turns Fran around and wastes no time removing the gorgeous gown, her sole focus on making sure the fire in Fran's eyes continues to burn. Fran's nimble fingers strip

Clarke of her couture just as quickly. Soon they unite in a full body embrace as their lips meld together once more.

"Clarke, darling. I want you to, I want—" Fran breaks away and advances to the closet. Returning swiftly, Fran drops in front of Clarke. "Please use this on me." Clarke looks down as she feels a harness sliding up her legs. Fran pants as she fits the device properly. Clarke feels a rush of desire course through her at the thought of being the dominant lover tonight. It's rare for her to control the pace of their lovemaking, particularly since Fran doesn't like giving up control. This show of trust pushes her ardor higher. She'll make sure Fran doesn't regret this decision.

Fran walks backward toward the bed while holding Clarke's hands. She murmurs Clarke's name while reclining on the bed, spreading her legs as a blatant invitation. Hardly believing what is occurring, Clarke crawls forward until she can position herself over Fran, gratified by the moan that floats through the air. With a wicked smile, Clarke sets out to ravish Fran. She never wants her to forget this night.

Settling between Fran's legs, she refrains from entering her. Instead, she rocks against Fran slowly while sucking forcefully on her neck. Not wanting to leave a mark, Clarke moves back up to capture those appealing lips, nibbling the lower one until Fran moans louder. Clarke rubs her tongue against Fran's before licking the top of her mouth. Her whimpers fuel Clarke's hunger, who sucks on her tongue and allows her fingers to dance along Fran's ribcage.

Palming Fran's belly, Clarke dips her head to capture a rock-hard nipple. She feels Fran tossing her head back as her fingers comb through Clarke's hair. They rock together, as Fran tilts her pelvis to welcome Clarke inside. She rubs Fran's clitoris with fingers dampened by the proof of Fran's desire, ripping a surprised shout from her. Clarke smiles as she licks at the other breast. She feels Fran's hands pulling on her hips, urging her to enter her body. Bracing her hands on either side of Fran's torso, Clarke angles herself before surging forward. They both groan at the sensation of their bodies melding together.

"God, you are so sexy." Clarke says these words while rocking her body enough to work the toy into Fran's body more without hurting her. Fran widens her legs, and Clarke moves her hips in a circular motion that makes Fran's body tremble. Restless hands travel across her back as Clarke pulls back enough that only the tip remains inside. Pushing forward again, she grunts with the effort to not push faster, push harder. She says in a breathless voice, "You are irresistible."

"Please, please." Although Fran's begging fills the room, Clarkes refuses to acquiesce. She's thought about this, about using this toy on Fran. As she continues to torture her with the slow, steady pace, Fran's ramblings become more urgent. "Clarke, what are you doing to me? I need you, darling." Fran's legs wrap around her waist, opening herself up and allowing Clarke to sink in further.

Feeling her control slip as her swollen clitoris rubs against Fran's, Clarke shudders. Gazing into fevered eyes, she marvels at the lust so apparent. Fran's mouth surrounds Clarke's breast, sucking greedily. Not able to hold back any longer, she thrusts faster, loving how Fran meets her body with a forceful counterpoint. Fingers dig into her shoulders as Clarke slants her hips upward and pushes. Fran shouts out her pleasure. Noting the reaction, Clarke keeps the angle, moving faster and faster. Sweat rolls down her back, as she strains to fuck Fran into oblivion.

It looks like she just might do it, too. Tremors are overtaking Fran's body, as she pulls Clarke closer. Clarke drops her head to kiss Fran, gasping as she does her best to keep their lips locked. Finding it too difficult, she tucks her head into Fran's neck and tilts her hips up more before thrusting hard. Hearing a high-pitched screech, Clarke keeps the grueling pace, loving the slapping of their bodies, the sparks behind her eyes, and the whimpers littering the room. She feels Fran arch into her as she releases a primal shout. Hands pull at Clarke's ass, keeping the pace constant as Fran breaks apart beneath her.

Clarke pulls her head back enough to watch, mesmerized, as Fran rides wave after wave of her orgasm, her body melting into a twitching mess once the aftershocks fade. Fran, with a hand thrown over her eyes, sweat-drenched hair, and glistening body, is stunning. Clarke licks at the perspiration on Fran's top lip, humming at the smile it elicits, and pulls out the toy before plopping down next to her. She's extremely aroused and in desperate need of release, but she is also astounded by what has just occurred. For the first time since they have been together, it appears Fran has passed out. Clarke is proud of herself.

She thinks about the birthday surprise she's preparing for Fran as her eyes travel over her resting form. Although she hasn't shared her poems with Fran, she's decided to gather all the ones she's written about her and combine them into a handmade leather journal. She's even commissioned someone to pen them in calligraphy. She's under no delusions that the poems are particularly good, but she's sure Fran will appreciate her willingness to reveal herself in this way. One of the poems reminds her of their lovemaking. She's titled it "Thunderstorms."

Thunderstorms: God's passion expressed,
Heralding brewing passions,
Rippling the water like a lover's touch down the arm.
Crackling energy: sexual tension,
Pulling the air taut with an undeniable connection.
Rain's scent: lovers' perfume,
Thickening the air with heady anticipation.
Thunder: a lover's cry,
Ripping across the night's silence.
Deluge: love's release,
Gentling the rain, and
Slowing breaths.
The air emanates the storm's aftermath.

Their lovemaking is heady. It changes the world around her. It sweetens every breath she takes. It makes her crave each inhalation that leads her to a future shared with Fran.

Resting her head on an arm, Clarke spends some time gazing at this lioness. Her lioness. How wonderful that she has so much more to learn about her. She's gorgeous. Clarke is in awe. She smiles tenderly when Fran removes her hand, eyelids fluttering open to reveal hazy blue eyes. A weak hand cups Clarke's chin, guiding her lips to waiting ones.

"That was magnificent. You are magnificent." Fran's voice is raspy, her voice practically gone from all her shouting.

Clarke feels relief flow through her. She's surprised to find that she enjoyed being the aggressor. Being in control, stripping Fran of her formidable presence, was exhilarating. Clarke could feel how evenly matched they are. Even better, she could feel Fran's trust.

They kiss again, taking their time to explore. Fran urges Clarke to lie on her back, her hands mapping Clarke's torso while following the trail with her lips. Clarke feels the passion overwhelming her again as Fran's talented hands guide her toward her own climax. Her joyful shout echoes throughout the room.

Before Clarke can recover her wits, she feels Fran cover her body. Staring at Fran in admiration, Clarke grasps her hips as she sinks onto the dildo. Fran begins to undulate seductively while focusing on Clarke's eyes, captivating her.

Fran meets each upward thrust of Clarke's hips vigorously by grinding downward, then lifting her body in counterpoint. She rocks fluidly, eyes closing as she becomes lost in the throes of ecstasy. When Clarke moves one hand to manipulate Fran's bundle of nerves, her eyes fly open as an orgasm takes her by surprise. "Clarke!" Throwing her head back, Fran releases a rich laugh as she rides Clarke.

Feeling another climax waiting in the wings, Clarke speeds up, the bewitching feeling of Fran rubbing against her pushing her into waves of bliss. Worn out, Clarke releases Fran's hips and gasps for air. A hot body settles next to her a moment later. "God, I love you." Clarke can feel her body becoming heavier even as her soul feels lighter.

"I love you, Clarke. You are by far the sexiest woman I have ever met." Fran delivers an exhausted though heartfelt kiss before curling into Clarke's body. "What you do to me."

Clarke hopes she will always spur Fran into such declarations.

***

Clarke nervously taps on her desk with her pen as she stares sightlessly at her computer screen. Today is Fran's birthday. Wanting to make it memorable, Clarke has made every effort to impress her. She may not be able to bring Fran to the best restaurants or shower her with gifts, but she's nothing if not inventive. Armed with Fran's schedule, she's left roses and poems in various places for her to find. They reflect how her feelings have developed from the first day they met to now. Wringing her hands, Clarke hopes Fran likes them.

She isn't the best poet. She knows that. She thought about creating animation or at least drawing some images for Fran, but she's enjoyed the challenge of writing poems, of expressing her deepest emotions through her words. She views it in the same vein as writing the narrative for a game. To draw in the gamer, she must use words to spark the imagination and set the tone. Even if her poems aren't the best, she hopes Fran appreciates the feelings behind them.

Wanting to make sure nothing ruins their evening, Clarke is splurging on dinner. She's picking it up on her way home. Fran has assured her that she'll be home on time. After dinner, Clarke plans to massage away all of Fran's stress before making love to her. She would have preferred to do more, but they're leaving in two days to visit her parents for Thanksgiving, and their schedules are jammed as a result.

Flicking her eyes toward the phone, Clarke scowls. Harry's text confirms that Fran received the final poem. Clarke presses her lips together. She doesn't understand why she's so anxious. Even if Fran believes the poems are juvenile, she will appreciate the effort involved. *Right?*

If Clarke is honest, though, she must admit it's not just the birthday plans which have her agitated. In two days, she will see her parents for the first time since she walked out on them in a high-scale restaurant four months ago. The night Fran asked her to move in. Her parents objected to the move, of course, but they hadn't seemed surprised. It made Clarke wonder what the conversation between Fran and her parents after she left was all about.

Refocusing on her work, she concentrates on the graphics of the main character's facial expressions. It takes a mammoth amount of attention to finish it. Clicking save, she dares to look at the clock. *Shit!* Shutting down her computer and packing it up, she calls the restaurant to make sure the food will be ready and hightails it out of Haboob, glad she doesn't run into Fran returning from an outside meeting.

Once home, Clarke sets up the bedroom with flowers, candles, and cues-up music to provide the proper ambiance for the massage. Dragging the massage table to their bedroom from its usual home in the guest bedroom, where Fran receives biweekly treatments, Clarke spends precious minutes trying to figure out how to adjust it to a height which will work for her. Clarke lays out the sheets and oil with care. Satisfied, she returns downstairs to prepare the dining room for their meal.

Twenty minutes later Clarke hears Fran's arrival. "Clarke?"

"In here." Clarke hurries to light the tapers in the candelabra and blows out the match. Clarke holds her breath when Fran stops short to take in the romantic display. Clarke smiles. "Hi."

"Hello." Cocking her head, Fran gazes at Clarke for several moments before walking toward her. "This is beautiful." Fran rests a hand on Clarke's collarbone as she leans forward to kiss her. "Thank you, darling."

"It's nothing. Certainly, less than what you deserve." Clarke smiles apologetically. "I'll do better next year."

"Don't be absurd." Although the words are harsh, the tone of voice is affectionate. "What you've done has made me feel so special, so privileged that I am having trouble finding the words to adequately thank you."

"Well. Now you know how I felt when I received the laptop." Clarke ignores how low her voice sounds and blinks repeatedly, not wanting to let her emotions get the better of her. This night is for Fran. The air between them has become thick with meaning. Clearing her throat, Clarke guides Fran to a chair and holds it out. "Madam, if it pleases you, kindly rest on this comfortable chair while dinner is served."

Fran's lips curl in amusement as she sits down. Clarke pours the wine and serves the appetizers before seating herself. She's pleased that Fran seems to be unwinding. Clarke can practically see the cords of stress falling off Fran as they flirt. Clarke purposefully steers their conversation away from work and her family. She wants Fran to relax. Clarke caters to Fran throughout the meal, hopping up whenever she needs something. Bending over to refill Fran's glass of wine, a hand on her arm stalls her.

"Clarke. This has been lovely."

"Oh, but this isn't all. As soon as we finish dinner, you have one hell of a massage waiting for you." Clarke grins at Fran's surprised look. After they finish their wine, Clarke leads Fran to their bedroom. Opening the door, Clarke follows Fran in and lights the candles. "I'll give you a few minutes to undress. Lie on your stomach, please." She delivers a chaste kiss before turning on the music and closing the door. Five minutes later she reenters to find Fran resting comfortably.

Over the next ninety minutes Clarke rubs out every knot she can find. She may not be a massage therapist, but she knows Fran's body well. By the time she finishes, Fran is purring. Gazing at Fran's serene face, Clarke feels her heart lurch. She's lovely. Like this, Fran appears much younger and more carefree. Clarke loves that she's able to evoke such reactions. Running her hand lightly from toes to head, Clarke ends the session with a very unprofessional kiss on the forehead. As Clarke moves away, she feels arms pulling her back for a long, intense kiss. "Make love to me, Clarke."

As if there is any doubt. As if mirroring the first time they made love, this time it is Clarke who kisses every inch of Fran's body reverently. It is Clarke who whispers how much she wants her, needs her. It is Clarke who kisses Fran again and again as if she can never get enough. She can't.

When she enters Fran, she feels more than hears Fran moan as she climaxes. Clarke kisses down Fran's body and feasts on its passionate outpouring, sucking on the labia with abandon before focusing on the sensitive bundle of nerves. Clarke does not relent until Fran screams her next release. Only then does Clarke take Fran into her arms. They remain in this position long enough for Clarke to dream of sensual fingers dancing across her abdomen and dipping into her wetness. Moving her body to the compelling rhythm, Clarke does not realize she isn't dreaming until an orgasm crashes over her. Clarke opens her mouth to exhale as she tilts her head back. Lips kiss her sternum lovingly while those magical fingers play with her breasts.

"Oh, Fran." Clarke sighs as she opens her eyes. A full smile and dancing eyes greet her. "Happy birthday."

"Indeed. If your animation endeavors fall short, I believe you could have a promising future as my personal massage therapist."

Clarke grins. "I'll take that as a compliment."

"As it was meant. Of course, your poems are quite exceptional, too. Publishable, even."

"No way. Those are only meant for your eyes." Clarke blushes with embarrassment. Some of those poems are very raw, so raw she has a challenging time reading them. "However, I was hoping you liked them enough to want to read them again." She rises to retrieve the leather-bound journal that she's wrapped for the occasion. She hands it to Fran, and settles next to her, hoping Fran will appreciate the effort that went into creating the collection of poems, and the courage she's drawn on to have them memorialized in this way.

Once Fran opens the gift, she takes her time to skim through the pages, a soft smile on her face. She stops at different poems, ones she hasn't seen before, and reads them. Her face is a kaleidoscope of emotions—running the gauntlet from amused to sorrowful to joyful. When she finally looks up, her lashes are wet with tears, emphasizing the bright blue of her eyes. "These are beautiful. I don't think I'll ever have the words to express how much these mean to me. Thank you." Fran delivers a tender kiss to Clark, who is so relieved that she could cry.

"The more I learn about you, the deeper I fall in love. Artist, poet, massage therapist, lover extraordinaire—I am extremely fortunate." Fran's face lights up as she smiles, her dancing eyes alerting Clarke that she's recovered from their earlier lovemaking. "I hope you aren't too tired, darling. It is still my birthday, and I'm craving something sweet to sate my voracious appetite."

As the sexual tension builds and the air thickens, Clarke arches into Fran's wandering hands, moaning her consent. And it's as simple as that.

The End.

About Jazzy Mitchell

Jazzy Mitchell is the proud publisher of Launch Point Press and on the founding Board of Directors for OPUS Literary Alliance. Jazzy's the author of four other contemporary lesbian fiction novels: *Lost Treasures*—which received an Honorable Mention for the 2016 Rainbow Awards, *Musings of a Madwoman*, *You Matter*, and *Undertow*. Jazzy lives in Portland, Oregon, with her beloved wife, three vivacious children, and small in body but huge in spirit, five-pound puppy.

Connect with Jazzy

Facebook – JazzyMitchellauthor

Email –publisher@launchpointpress.com

Website – www.launchpointpress.com

Note to Readers:

Thank you for reading a book from Launch Point Press. We have made every effort to edit this book. However, typos do slip in. If you find an error in the text or formatting, please email is at publisher@launchpointpress.com so the issue can be corrected.

We appreciate you as a reader and want to ensure you enjoy the reading process. We would like you to consider posting a review on your preferred media sites and/or your blog or website.

For more information on upcoming releases, author interviews, contests, giveaways and more, please sign up for our newsletter and visit us as at Launch Point Press: www.launchpointpress.com and "Like" us on Facebook: Launch Point Press.

Bright Blessings